Holding the reins more loosely, she looked at the screen and swiped it.

"We're almost there," she said. "Let's head a little to our right. Whatever's causing the dot to appear in my GPS tracker is just over that hill." She pointed somewhat ahead but unsurprisingly toward their right.

"No further indication of what it is?" Casey had to ask, even knowing that greater detail, even close by, was highly unlikely on a GPS map.

"Nope, though it's likely to be a cow—or just the GPS tag that's somehow been taken off. We'll find out soon."

And they did. The result clearly upset Melody. A lot.

For as soon as their horses walked over the small ridge nearest the dot's location and they could see the grass-covered part of the hillside beyond, the cow that was wearing the tag was visible.

Lying there on the ground.

Clearly dead.

* * *

Dear Reader,

This is my first book in the Colton series, but it won't be my last. I'm excited to join the many wonderful authors who have contributed to the Colton books.

Colton 911: Caught in the Crossfire is the first of two books featuring the Coltons of Cactus Creek. In this book, Deputy Sheriff Casey Colton is directed by his boss, the sheriff, to help find a dozen highly valuable cattle stolen from OverHerd Ranch owned by the town selectman. Lovely ranch hand Melody Hayworth shows him where the fence was damaged to let the cattle out on the range. Together, on horseback, they follow the rustled cattle's trail for several days. Both of them have a job to do—save the missing cattle. Both have recently been involved in bad relationships, so surely nothing will come of their togetherness...or will it?

I hope you enjoy *Colton 911: Caught in the Crossfire*. Please come visit me at my website, killerhobbies. blogspot.com. And, yes, I'm on Facebook, too.

Linda O. Johnston

COLTON 911: CAUGHT IN THE CROSSFIRE

Linda O. Johnston

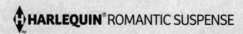

Special thanks and acknowledgment are given to Linda O. Johnston for her contribution to the Colton 911 miniseries.

Recycling programs for this product may not exist in your area.

ISBN-13: 978-1-335-66222-4

Colton 911: Caught in the Crossfire

Copyright © 2019 by Harlequin Books S.A.

www.Harlequin.com

Printed in U.S.A.

Linda O. Johnston loves to write. While honing her writing skills, she worked in advertising and public relations, then became a lawyer...and enjoyed writing contracts. Linda's first published fiction appeared in *Ellery Queen's Mystery Magazine* and won a Robert L. Fish Memorial Award for Best First Mystery Short Story of the Year. Linda now spends most of her time creating memorable tales of paranormal romance, romantic suspense and mystery. Visit her on the web at www.lindaojohnston.com.

Books by Linda O. Johnston

Harlequin Romantic Suspense

Colton 911

Colton 911: Caught in the Crossfire

K-9 Ranch Rescue

Second Chance Soldier
Trained to Protect

Undercover Soldier
Covert Attraction

Harlequin Nocturne

Alpha Force

Alpha Wolf
Alaskan Wolf
Guardian Wolf
Undercover Wolf
Loyal Wolf
Canadian Wolf
Protector Wolf

Back to Life

Visit the Author Profile page at Harlequin.com for more titles.

To my wonderful husband, Fred. Of course.

Chapter 1

Casey Colton dashed up the large stairway from the first floor of the sheriff's department building in Sur County, Arizona. As deputy sheriff, he was used to taking orders, but the curt phone call he'd just received from his boss, Jeremy Krester, was more of a command. Jeremy was usually fairly laid-back, so that worried Casey.

"Hi, Bob," he said as he entered Jeremy's outer office, not stopping behind the desk stacked with folders but swerving around toward the door behind it.

Apparently Bob Andrews, a fellow deputy, had been informed of his pending presence. "Go on in," said the young, wide-eyed guy, who was wearing a beige uniform that matched the one Casey wore. "Sheriff Krester's expecting you."

As Casey knew well.

He reached out, turned the doorknob and hurried inside. And stopped near the doorway. Sheriff Krester wasn't alone.

Of course, Casey had expected to see his tall, thin, gray-haired boss sitting at the desk facing the door of the sizable office. He wore a similar uniform to Casey's, too, but with a lot more decorations than the normal colorful shoulder patches of the Sur County Sheriff's Department. And his badge was even more prominently displayed on his chest.

But the other guy? That was a surprise.

So was the fact that he paced the wood floor and only stopped for an instant as Casey entered, barely maneuvering around him before continuing.

It was Clarence Edison, the town selectman of Cactus Creek. He was dressed in a suit, as he usually was, and was all business.

In his late sixties, Clarence hadn't gone completely gray but still had more darkness in his hair than Jeremy. He'd been a selectman for many years, but he was known just as much—maybe even more—for owning the successful OverHerd Ranch, outside of town, where he raised Angus cattle. Casey had only seen the large ranch when driving by it.

And, yes, its name—OverHerd—was intended to be a pun, he'd been informed. Not that he was surprised. The selectman was a kidder, someone who liked keeping things light. Casey had noted some of that, too, when he'd attended city meetings, where Clarence got people laughing at times—possibly to make other government officials or even local citizens lighten up. And, therefore, do things his way.

Casey had met Clarence now and then at various town events when the sheriff's department helped to keep things civil and in order. He seemed like a nice guy. He was smart and enjoyed being in charge and talking to large groups, even having fun with them.

But what was he doing here now? And why was he pacing that way?

"Sit down," Jeremy ordered Casey as he waved at one of the three chairs facing his cluttered desk. Jeremy also glanced at Clarence, but his expression toward the selectman appeared to be more of a suggestion than a command.

Casey obeyed as he eyed his boss without looking at the town elder. His curiosity increased even more but he couldn't push things. Not with these two men, who were both used to being in charge.

But it didn't take long for Clarence to start talking even as he did deign to take a seat, and then turned his chair to face Casey.

"Need your help, Deputy," Clarence growled in a low voice Casey hadn't heard before, his blue eyes intense. "I understand you helped catch a cattle rustler a couple months ago."

Was that what this was about? But what had Jeremy told him? "That's right, although it wasn't a big deal. There were only a few cattle involved—one bull and two cows. And it turned out it was a family-feud kind of situation."

Noting some movement from the corner of his eye,

Casey turned and saw Jeremy making a slight throat-cutting gesture—in other words, he was telling Casey to shut up about that event.

"Ahh," Jeremy said with a clearly forced smile on his narrow face. "Our deputy there is being a bit modest. Yes, it did turn out to be a family problem, but the members whose cattle disappeared didn't know that at first, and neither did we. Casey figured it out—and found the missing cattle. There were some charges brought against the thieving relatives but they talked it through and paid for some of our time and…well, it's all resolved now, and they're back to being okay."

"Okay," Clarence repeated. He, too, had turned to face the sheriff. "You won't find anything similar in my situation, though."

"No," Jeremy said. "There's a lot more involved. Why don't you tell Deputy Colton about it?" He nodded to the selectman, then looked back at Casey.

He was right, Casey thought as Clarence filled him in. This situation didn't sound nearly as simple as the one Casey had helped with before. For one thing, it involved the disappearance of a dozen cows, not just three. And they were Angus cows being used to procreate, to increase the number of cattle at the ranch and for sale to other ranches.

Very valuable Angus cows. Each was worth thousands of dollars.

No wonder Clarence was upset.

"I want you to act quickly," he continued. "One good thing is that I've had all the cattle tagged with GPS, but the terrain doesn't work for cars, and helicopters or planes couldn't land there. Seeing anything like that could cause the rustlers to kill the cattle and run, anyway. Even drones could scare them into doing something bad. They seem to be on the move so we can't pinpoint where they are for you to send a whole team in to get them. Not yet, at least. And—"

Casey heard a buzzing sound. Clarence pulled a phone out of his pocket and looked at it, then listened.

After a minute he said, "Damn. I need to head back to my office right now for an important meeting. I want someone from here who knows what he's doing to get to my ranch right away. A couple of ranch hands are there and can show you around and explain what happened and when." He stood and began pacing between Casey and his superior's desk again. He looked at Casey. "Since you've solved one rustling case lately, even though it's not quite the same thing, I agree with Sheriff Krester that it makes sense for you to go and scope things out. Maybe even solve it on the spot." His grin toward Casey was wide, though his eyes narrowed and remained skeptical.

Casey asked, "Any people you think might be the rustlers—family members or not?"

"Not," Clarence said strongly. "I trust my family—but that didn't stop me from notifying the local members by phone and listening to their shock and sympathy. And analyzing it. I've no reason to suspect any of them. Besides…"

He paused, looked from Casey toward the sheriff, then back again.

"Besides what?" Jeremy prompted, as Casey believed was appropriate, considering the way Clarence had spoken and looked at him.

"Besides, the dozen cattle of mine that were stolen were all very valuable females. Cows." He paused. "So that tells me that whoever did it was one hell of a *cow*ard." All three of them laughed at the emphasis he placed on the first syllable—briefly and not particularly hilariously.

"Well, let me at him. Or her." Casey stood directly in front of the selectman. "I won't allow whoever it is to cow me. I'll do my damnedest to figure this out soon and get your cattle back."

Melody Hayworth pulled opened the front door of the main house of OverHerd Ranch before the doorbell finished chiming.

She'd been waiting inside uncomfortably, along with Pierce Tostig, one of the other ranch hands, since their boss had called half an hour ago.

It was midafternoon. Earlier, a couple of the other hands had headed out toward the pasture where one of the herds of special, valuable Angus cattle had supposedly spent the night and morning, as usual…but they hadn't found them there. Using the GPS apps on their phones, they'd confirmed that the geotagged cows were now far away, somewhere still on the ranch, but heading toward its outer edges. It appeared that the fence had been partly destroyed, apparently by rustlers, and the cows had gotten out. Those hands had called Clarence, who'd expressed concern not only about the missing stock, but also about those that remained. He'd insisted that all of the ranch hands—or at least most of them—find and protect the rest.

He'd also said he'd get the authorities involved, and then ordered that a couple of employees—Pierce Tostig and Melody—should stick around to help and advise the sheriff's department when someone from there arrived at the ranch, then stay involved in finding those missing cattle.

Now, Melody said "Please come in" to the man in uniform who stood there—a deputy sheriff, according to the patch on his upper left sleeve.

"Thanks." He immediately held out his hand for a shake after she shut the door. "I'm Deputy Casey Colton," he said. "I was sent here by Selectman Clarence Edison because—"

"Because some of our—*his*—cattle have been rustled," Melody interrupted. She had no need to wait for any further introductions, but she noticed that his grip was strong and somehow sexy, which was irrelevant. Her boss had made it clear in his phone call that she and the others were to give the deputy who showed up all the information they had about the rustling situation. And to show him where the cattle had been located, and how they'd apparently gotten out…with help.

"Let's go in here first," she said to Deputy Colton, gesturing for him to follow her through the attractively decorated wooden entryway into the adjoining living room. Melody considered the decor a bit overdone, but it worked well for a ranch house owned by someone as revered—and rich—as her boss.

She watched the deputy's face as he looked around.

The guy was good-looking, and not just because he wore that uniform. His hair was brown and cut relatively short. His matching eyebrows over dazzling blue eyes were nicely arched and his chin was slightly prominent. He had some light facial hair, maybe surprising because of his job. But it looked good on him.

In fact, every part of his appearance was eye-catching—and Melody could have kicked herself for even noticing.

The only thing important about this guy was whether he could find the missing cattle.

For now, his boots rapped on the portion of the wooden floor not covered by an antique gold-and-brown area rug. The deputy approached Pierce, who stood near one of the windows at the far side of the room beside the stone fireplace.

Heading toward them, Pierce was dressed even more casually than Melody's typical blue denim work shirt, jeans and black boots with tight laces. He wore an oversize, short-sleeved white T-shirt and overly faded jeans—fashionable, perhaps, but it seemed as if there were more holes than denim.

"Hi," the deputy said, stopping near the side of the ornate brown leather sofa set that dominated the room's seating arrangement. He introduced himself to Pierce, as he'd done with Melody, and was clearly taking charge of this meeting. "Can we sit down? I want to hear everything about the missing cattle—where they were, who discovered they were gone. Everything."

"Yeah, I figured." Pierce plopped down on one of the two-seater portions of the sofa set. Ears protruded from wavy hair clipped close on the sides of his head. He was around forty, like Melody, and was clean-shaven with blue eyes. Pierce was okay-looking and mostly genial, but perhaps not as hard a worker as he should be.

Melody took a seat on the similar sofa section, while the deputy sat on the larger one and leaned forward, his elbows on his knees. He looked toward her as if encouraging her to begin the description.

But Pierce took over. Pointing toward the rear of the house, he described the five-hundred-acre ranch and about how many cattle there were—quite a few more than those that were stolen, fortunately. "Our main range is out that way. It's divided into sections because of the terrain. Dry sand in some areas, grass and higher growth in others, lots of hillsides, small mountains, all that kind of thing."

"Interesting," the deputy said. "I'll want to see it soon, or as much of it as possible. Now, tell me more about who discovered the problem and how."

Again he looked toward Melody. Pierce attempted to answer, never mind that Deputy Colton seemed to be addressing her. But as much as she liked Pierce and the way he mostly helped her learn about this ranch, Melody disliked being ignored. She spoke up, talking over Pierce.

"As it turns out, I probably should have been the one to discover the problem, but I wasn't." She described how she and some ranch hands, including Pierce, resided in apartments in the bunkhouse behind this house and slightly west of the stables. The fenced-in ranch land began behind them, and the several herds of cattle ranged in different fenced areas within it.

Last night, she hadn't slept well, although she wasn't sure why. "Now, though, I believe I might have heard something in the distance while asleep that disturbed me, though I didn't fully awaken."

"I'll want to see the location of your residences, particularly yours," the lawman said.

"Of course, Deputy Colton." From what she'd learned, the name *Colton* was an important one in many areas. Whether or not he was a lawman, though, she didn't particularly like his knowing where she lived.

"Just call me Casey," the law-enforcement official said with a small grin on that good-looking face. As uncomfortable as she felt, she knew that getting along with him, including being on a first-name basis, was probably going to be helpful in the long run as they worked with him to find the missing cattle.

"Okay, Casey. And as you know, I'm Melody."

"And I'm Pierce," the other man said. "Are we all going to head to bed together now?"

Melody found herself laughing, even as the discomfort within her eased a bit. "Not I," she said.

"Only if the missing cattle are there," Casey retorted. "So, okay, tell me more about how you discovered that those cattle were missing." He smiled at Pierce first, then her. "And we'll keep our minds on the range, not in the bedroom."

"Fine with me," Melody said with a shake of her head. Although the idea of combining Casey and a bedroom… She forced the thought out of her head.

"Well, if that's the case," Pierce said, "I'm out of here. I'm supposed to be out in the east pasture with a couple of the other hands but thought I was needed here." He stood, nodded toward Casey and said, "Hope you find those missing cows soon. Real soon." And then he left.

So, no matter what Clarence said, apparently Pierce wasn't staying involved.

"I second what he said," Melody told Casey. "And though I can tell you a lot more about this place, I think it'll be more productive if we go outside and I show you around."

"Fine," Casey said. "I'll want to see everything you and the others have found so far before I really dig into the investigation."

"Sure," Melody said. "I've only worked here for about six months, but I've learned a lot about this great ranch. And although I haven't gone chasing those missing cattle yet, we can go to the place they got past the OverHerd fencing and start our real investigation there."

They both stood and she looked at Casey. He had an odd expression on his face. A scowl, she thought, and it seemed to mar his good looks.

What was he thinking? she wondered. Good thing he was scowling, though. He clearly wasn't having the same kinds of thoughts about her as she had about him.

Although… Well, not going to happen.

It was better that way.

Chapter 2

Our real investigation? Casey didn't want to contradict Melody, not when he needed her to show him what she and the others had found so far, but she wasn't going to be part of *his* investigation.

He was the deputy assigned here. This was his job.

And besides…well, he was finding it a bit uncomfortable to be around Melody, especially now, when they were alone.

Problem was, she seemed much too beautiful to be a ranch hand. Her long, dark hair was secured behind her head in a ponytail, and she had a gorgeous face, with deep brown eyes above high cheekbones and below attractively curved, dark eyebrows. Those eyes showed what she appeared to be feeling—sometimes infuriated by the rustling that had gone on here, sometimes amused, or irritated, by what Pierce had said, sometimes pleading with Casey to fix the problem…and always winsome and appealing.

Too appealing. Never mind that she appeared to be a little older than him.

And since he'd been left at the altar four years ago, he hadn't been interested in another woman.

Didn't want to be now.

But he needed information from her. So—

"Great," he said. "Let's go."

He glanced around again before beginning to follow her out the door. The sofa from which he'd risen, which matched the other seats, had been surprisingly comfortable considering how elaborate it was, with its leather seating punched evenly with deep matching buttons and back lined with attractive, carved wood. It looked expensive. Everything in this room—everything he'd seen at this ranch—looked expensive. But then, he didn't doubt that Clarence Edison could afford all that and more.

Though perhaps not as much if he didn't get back his valuable missing cattle.

Melody, hips swaying gently even as she hurried, led him in a different direction down the hallway they'd walked along before, and soon they passed through the large kitchen, which was also elaborately outfitted with expensive-looking equipment, though no one was working there now. Did Edison have a personal chef? He wouldn't be surprised.

Soon they were on the varnished wooden porch, having exited from the rear door. The yard beyond was mostly dirt decorated with desert plants, cacti and more.

Straight ahead, past the elongated stables and an even larger barn with a peaked roof, a mountain range rose, not especially tall but broad. Another building, possibly a bunkhouse, was located near the back of the ranch house. Toward the south, beyond the substantial-looking fence, was land covered with grass, as far as he could see. He couldn't tell how large the vast rolling lawn was, but judging by what he understood of the ranch's success, it probably went on for many miles.

"I don't think you need to see the insides of the buildings, at least not now," Melody said. "The stable houses our horses, of course. We ranch hands usually ride them when we're heading out into the pastures to observe and take care of the grazing herds. The cattle don't spend much time in the barn, although the cows sometimes do when they're calving, or if there's any indication of illness. For now, we could ride out to the pastures on horseback, but I think you'll get a better sense of the pasture if we just walk this time. Okay?"

"Fine," Casey said. It would be a good idea for him to borrow a horse when he'd learned the basics and was ready to start his real investigation, but for now he would learn best if he took the time to walk around and look at everything he could from that perspective. As long as— "But you will take me to the fenced area where the cattle escaped, won't you?"

"Absolutely," Melody said. "All the hands are aware of it, and have seen the damage to the fence there, too. The other herds are now within different fenced areas so they can't disappear that way, too."

"Fine."

"And in case our boss didn't tell you, the cows are all branded with a logo that says 'OHR' for OverHerd Ranch. Even more important, they're all equipped with GPS trackers. But the terrain out there isn't appropriate for driving out to find them, so all we have so far is an accurate idea which way they went."

"Yes, he mentioned that. Thanks." Not surprising that the ranch hands were up-to-date—but it was a bit surprising that apparently no one had used the technology to go after the cattle yet.

Although it was a better thing that they hadn't, if rustlers were involved. Law enforcement was his job, not theirs.

For now, he found himself smiling slightly in amusement as the slender and clearly physically fit Melody hurried off in front of him, as she undoubtedly wanted to reach the pasture that usually contained the cattle—when they weren't missing. He hurried, too, to catch up with her and stay by her side. He began asking questions about the landscape, the types of plants and the topography, which was flat at first but he saw rolling ridges in the near background.

She climbed quickly over the portion of the long, substantial-looking fence that was chest-high to her, a bit less to him. The way she scaled it agilely made it appear as if she practiced daily. Maybe she did. And he told himself again to quit noticing such things.

His mind landed briefly on his ex-fiancée, Georgia. He and his fraternal twin brother, Everett, had known her from childhood And Everett's best friend had been Sean Dodd, Georgia's brother, but she'd dumped Casey.

But enough of that. He had important things to think about now. As he had to do too often, even now, he eliminated Georgia from his thoughts.

The weather was typical for this time of year—November—in this part of Arizona. It was sometimes warm but far from scorching, though it often grew cooler, especially at night. A nearly perfectly blue sky, no humidity. Nearly perfect.

Past the fence, as they both strode over the uneven, grassy ground, he asked what Melody knew about the ranch and its origins, just to make conversation until she got them to where she could show him something significant.

As Melody glanced sideways toward him, her long black ponytail swayed. "I can tell you what I heard, but I'm a relative newcomer here. The other hands have been here longer."

She wasn't looking at him now, but somehow her expression had hardened.

Where had she lived before? Why had she decided to become a ranch hand, and why here?

Was she unhappy about being the least experienced of the ranch hands here? He was highly curious all of a sudden, especially considering that oddly defensive look on her face. He asked, "So where did you come from? Is this your first job as a ranch hand?"

She again looked at him. Her brow creased and her mouth tightened. He assumed she was going to tell him where to go, to stop asking questions.

Maybe she didn't want to think of the past, either.

"Er... I'm sorry," he began, wanting to back off. "I didn't mean to be nosy."

But she responded...kind of. "I came from Texas. And, no, this isn't my first job as a ranch hand. I learned all about it there." She turned her attention toward where she was walking, as she should on this uneven area. "And one of the things I know well is that this kind of grass, this terrain, supports cattle well." She began a description of how she had studied different kinds of grasses and that these pastures seemed to incorporate several, although she wasn't certain. "Whatever they are, the grasses here seem to feed some pretty healthy cattle." She started talking about fescue and rye and stuff he really didn't care about, but she made it sound noteworthy.

"Interesting" was all he said. And in a way it was—considering the source.

He was finding Melody much too interesting... Which had to stop.

He started examining the topography more closely. It was flat in some areas, then rose to low hills and was flat again.

"Hey." Melody had suddenly stopped talking about grasses. "We're finally approaching where they got out."

She kept walking as she pointed out a spot in the distance...and then tripped. He instinctively reached out to grab her and hold her up, although he quickly realized she'd regained her balance on her own.

"Thanks," she said, anyway, her voice hoarse as she pulled her arm from his hand quickly. She immediately looked away from him and began to walk fast again.

He had an urge to hold her hand—to help her keep her balance. But that would be a bad idea.

A *very* bad idea.

He had a sense that if he tried it, he'd be the one to trip over his own feet and fall onto his knees.

And he'd be the one to look bad.

She was the ranch hand, not him. She could most likely wrangle a steer with her eyes closed. Even tie knots a lot better than him.

Instead of holding on to her, he'd take a different kind of advantage of her company now, since he'd be on his own for the actual investigation, at least initially, and possibly until another deputy or two was assigned to work with him. And being in Melody's presence... well, asking her questions related to what had happened here would be a whole lot easier for him than holding any other kind of conversation with her.

Like a flirtation? No way. There were no women in his life now. He didn't want any, despite how attractive she was. And especially not until he'd learned enough to be sure she wasn't involved in stealing the cattle.

So—who'd taken them, and why? They could certainly talk about that. It wasn't something he had much of a notion about on his own yet, not without investigating first—though he did have one potential suspect in mind that wasn't Melody.

According to local news, Edison's wife, Hilda, had left him last year and was no longer in town—or so Casey believed, but that didn't mean she was innocent. Hilda Edison was surely getting up in years, like her ex, so she probably couldn't have done this herself. But had she arranged for the rustling for her own financial gain, or revenge…or both?

Melody started responding to what he'd asked before, relaying her knowledge about the origins of OverHerd Ranch, which she had already admitted was limited since she'd moved here fairly recently. She understood that Clarence, who had grown up in Phoenix with a wealthy family, had moved to Cactus Creek after college and started the ranch. Then he'd married and he and his wife had a couple of kids, who were grown now and living elsewhere. She didn't know much about the ranch's development, which was fine since it probably had nothing to do with the current situation, although it might have been interesting to hear.

Casey could ask Clarence about that, if necessary, or maybe even look it up online. But for now, he interrupted gently and asked instead who she and the other ranch hands suspected in this, and why.

Unsurprisingly, she mentioned Hilda first. The other hands were already gossiping that their boss's ex might be involved. No one knew how much Hilda had gotten from the divorce, but if she didn't consider it enough, that could be a motive for her to steal some cattle.

Their kids? From what she'd gathered, Clarence had remained fairly generous with them, so while they were possible suspects, they didn't rank high on the others' lists.

Who else? Again, there were rumors, sometimes about political opponents or other townsfolk who didn't always agree with how Clarence ran things, but no one person stood out as having anything particularly against the man. No, the ranch hands seemed to think it was somewhat random.

"You might check in other areas around here to see if there've been other rustling situations lately, and if any of them seem at all similar," Melody said. A good idea, one he'd already thought of and would make sure Sheriff Krester had someone work on while Casey conducted his on-site investigation here.

"Will do" was all he said to Melody. And for the next few minutes both of them remained quiet. They were getting close to the clearly damaged fence, and Casey, at least, was studying the rolling hillside, mostly covered in grass and patches of other kinds of plant life, but with several other areas of bare soil. There were more pasture areas beyond the broken fence that seemed to stretch forever.

And no sign of cattle anywhere.

He glanced at his watch. It was nearing three o'clock. They'd been out for more than half an hour, and the walk back would also take that long. He wanted to spend some time at the broken-fence site first, too.

There would still be a few hours of daylight after their return, on this late fall day. Still, even if he found something around here, darkness might drop before he could deal with it. It would make more sense to return tomorrow. On horseback, maybe.

On his own, with whatever it took to track the cows' GPS signals.

Suddenly feeling the urge to stop wasting time and get to the fence already, Casey began sprinting forward. And he noticed that Melody was keeping up with him.

The fence consisted of oblong wooden stakes of moderate height, anchored into the ground, with three rows of straight metal piping connecting each pair of those stakes.

Here, though, four of the stakes had been knocked from their anchors and damaged, with gouges in the splintered wood indicating that some kind of tool had been used. The piping had been removed and stacked in rows off to the side. And the grassy ground beneath the opening was tamped down unevenly, as if cattle had walked through it—not a surprise.

This was clearly not some kind of accident or natural phenomenon. Someone had done it. Probably several someones, since removing the stakes could not have been easy.

Casey emitted a low whistle. "Wow. What a mess." He kneeled and started examining some of the splintered wood and the pipes, looking at the ground, as well.

"With no tools left here, either, to show how it was done," Melody said.

"Yeah," he responded. "I'll request that my department send someone here to check for fingerprints, but I suspect they won't find anything."

Melody nodded her pretty head as she kneeled beside him. "Anyone skilled enough to do this most likely has done something similar before—and knew to use gloves."

"Could be." He, of course, carried plastic gloves in his pocket for situations in which he didn't want to mess up any evidence, as well as a gun in his role as a deputy sheriff. "Well," he said, "I guess I could start looking for any evidence right here, but—"

"But here's what we should do," Melody interrupted. "Let's find those cattle. We can go on a stakeout on horseback—follow the cows, thanks to the way Clarence has made sure all his animals are tagged. Keep following them until we find them, even if it takes a few days and nights. And—"

It was Casey's turn to interrupt. "Sounds like a great idea." Of course, he'd already been considering it—though not exactly the way she said. "And I appreciate your offer, but I'll do it on my own, starting early tomorrow."

"Well, of course, I'll come with you," Melody insisted. "How well do you know how to ride a horse? I'll have to pick out one for you that matches your skills, though I can handle any of them, the faster the better. I'm damn good at it, so—"

"Now, wait a minute." Casey stood up quickly and stared down at Melody. She, too, rose and met his gaze. "I'd appreciate your allowing me to borrow one of the ranch's horses tomorrow, and maybe longer," he said to appease her. He continued, "I'll have to see how things go before rushing back to town, so as you suggested I might camp out for a night or two, depending on what I find—or don't find. But that's me. I'm the deputy assigned to handle this investigation, and I'll do it. *Myself.*"

Her expression turned into a glare, even as she put her hands on her hips. He noticed then that her nails were short and plain. No polish on them. No lipstick on her, either. Not that she needed anything like that to look pretty. But this way she looked more like the ranch hand she was.

"Then maybe you'd better bring your own horse," she told him coldly.

They both continued to glare at each other as his mind raced to try to figure out where he'd be able to get a horse on his own—and fast. Could he soothe her somehow in a way that ensured she'd still back off from interfering in his investigation?

She dropped her hands, even as she shook her head, a wry expression on that too-attractive face. "Look, Casey," she said—and for just then he'd have preferred her to refer to him as "Deputy Colton." "You're in charge of this investigation. I understand that. But I'll bet I can help you since I probably know this ranch, and cattle, better than you. Let's look around a little bit now and I'll try to convince you. But even if I don't, please let me join you tomorrow. I really give a damn about those missing cows, and I'll do everything I can to save them and bring them home."

He raised his head, just a little. "Look, Ms. Hayworth." He, at least, could return to formality. "It's one thing for me to be out there attempting to solve this apparent crime and to go after any perpetrators as well as the missing cattle. I'm trained to do such things. It's my job. But I don't want to have to worry about protecting you, too."

"Then don't worry about it. I'm volunteering. If anything happens to me, it's my own fault. And what if I really *can* help you?"

He recognized that this argument was going no-where. "We'll see," he responded, then he moved forward to the broken fence and maneuvered his way to the property beyond, intentionally ignoring his difficult companion for the moment.

But he couldn't really ignore her, especially when, a few feet away from him, she, too, edged her way to the far side beyond the broken fence. She started walking around, looking first into the distance, then glancing down to the ground. Then she did it again, even as Casey pretty much did the same thing.

And he saw some stuff that was interesting, like hoofprints in the grass, but unlikely to be any helpful evidence.

"Okay, Casey, look at this," Melody called to him. She gestured for him to join her, even as she continued studying the ground.

"Look at this," she repeated and pointed to an area right by her feet, where the grass had been tromped down and some dirt showed, similar to the ground he'd been examining, too. "See that? There are some hoofprints of cows, probably the missing ones since the prints are fairly new—sharp and prominent. They're heading in that direction." She pointed. "South. That's the way we should look for them."

Casey couldn't help himself. He laughed. "Guess what? Your cows left hoofprints over where I was standing, too, and I was studying them when you called me to come over."

Melody looked slightly abashed, but then her expression again became defiant. "Then, good. We're on the same page. We can compare and help each other and—"

"I understand you want to help and I appreciate it. But like I told you—"

"Look," she interrupted, "I know a lot more about cattle and hoofprints than you do. And more about the ranch and pastures, too." She was being a bit repetitious. He knew that, hadn't forgotten it. But still…

"I get all that," he told her. "And I've already told you why it's not a good idea for you to come."

"I'll prove otherwise," she insisted, contradicting him again. She began moving forward quickly, her head down.

But they weren't going to learn more now. Not here. Tomorrow he'd hurry in the same direction and hopefully find something helpful.

Maybe even those missing cattle…

"Hey. Look at that." Melody had stopped and was looking down to what was undoubtedly more cattle hoofprints. Only, she bent and reached for something, then stopped. She looked up at him again. "I doubt that any cow dropped that," she said.

"What?" he asked. He kneeled down beside her… and stared.

She was pointing to an area within a hoofprint, in dirt between fronds of tamped-down grass, and something small and shiny gleamed from it.

"What is that?" He resisted the urge to grab and examine it—and was glad she hadn't done that, either.

"It looks like some kind of silver charm," Melody responded in a somewhat hushed voice. "It could have been there before any cattle walked or stampeded around here through the fence during this rustling, but I've never seen anything like it in any of the pastures."

"I think," he mused, "and I may just be reaching for something helpful to identify some suspects and get this thing resolved, but you just might have found our first piece of evidence."

Chapter 3

Melody was impressed, though not surprised, when Casey took a couple of pictures with his cell phone, then pulled vinyl gloves from his pocket, picked up the charm and stuck it into a small plastic bag he also carried.

Clearly, he was prepared to do his job, wherever it led him and whatever evidence he happened to find.

The charm was the kind worn on necklaces or bracelets, and appeared to be silver. It was in the shape of the letter *G*.

"Does this look familiar to you?" He held the bag containing the charm toward Melody.

She shook her head. "Not at all."

But that inspired her to continue studying the ground

in that area, and Casey did, too. Neither of them found anything else other than more hoofprints.

"Do you think the charm was dropped by one of the rustlers?" Melody asked the deputy as they finally gave up.

"Anything's possible," he said with a shrug of his wide shoulders as he shot a wry look in her direction. A frustrated look. She wished she could do something— identify the charm, find something more helpful, to ease that frustration.

But she was frustrated, too. And no solution came to her.

"Let's head back now," he said, shoving the bag into his pocket. "Maybe we'll figure things out better tomorrow."

"Absolutely," she said, hoping it was true.

The walk back to the ranch house was a lot faster than the one to the damaged fence. But going in this direction, they didn't need to check for any indication of where the cattle were or who'd rustled them through that fence.

Or whether there were any more charms on the ground.

Not until tomorrow.

And, yes, she would be going along with Casey. It was important to her to do the best job possible here. This ranch had become her refuge after leaving her past behind, and she adored its cattle. She intended to help to save the stolen ones. Period.

She had to give Casey credit for not grumbling or protesting when she said, as they started back, "So I assume that, as the first person to find evidence in your crime investigation, I can come along tomorrow and continue to help you."

"I assume so," he said resignedly. He shot her a crooked sideways smile. "And, yeah, we can do the kind of stakeout you described."

She couldn't help smiling back and was careful not to make it appear she was gloating. Or at least not too much.

Besides, Casey was one good-looking guy, so it wasn't hard to smile at him.

Not that she had any intention of allowing her goal of helping to find the missing cattle by working with this guy turn into any kind of personal interest in him.

She'd learned her lesson not too long ago. It was why she had left her Texas home and found a job here, in Arizona, as a ranch hand, after her ugly, depressing divorce.

She knew now that it hadn't been the smartest thing to marry her high-school sweetheart, Travis Ellison, and follow him to Dallas. They'd only been married a couple of years before Travis, who'd become a big-city banker, had left her for a colleague, a much younger woman named Loretta Lane.

What had made it even more heartbreaking was that Travis had told Melody she was a "country girl," and he needed a "real woman."

Whatever that meant, it had hurt. A lot. She had sometimes suspected the worst about Travis before then, that he was cheating on her, but since she'd thought she loved him, she'd stayed with him, hoping they could work things out. At least she'd tried, but it had also hurt that he didn't seem to care.

That insult had finally led to the inevitable end of their relationship.

And, if being a skilled and happy ranch hand meant she was a country girl, then that was fine with her.

She realized she'd somehow sped up even more as she allowed her thoughts to go—as they often did these days—in that painful direction.

"Hey, what's your hurry?" Casey called as he caught up with her again. "Got a hot date tonight?"

She slowed a bit and turned to look into his face. His expression was teasing, yet she read some curiosity there, too. "Yeah, sure. With some horses. I need to make sure they're taken care of, and also want to figure out which'll be best on our stakeout."

"Right. Good idea. But you do understand, don't you, that I'm planning to stay out there till I—we—find those missing cattle? You can return to your place at the ranch anytime, of course, but—"

"And you'll love it if I quit, won't you? Well, don't count on it. I'm in this to win, too. Those cows…well, they're kind of my wards now. They're mine, though I don't own them and just care for them. That's my job and my vocation. And I'll do anything to bring them home safely." Including argue with him, to save the cattle she cared for.

She was surprised that Casey stopped walking, but she did, too. She couldn't quite interpret his expression, but he appeared impressed, somehow.

Or maybe that was what she hoped he felt.

"Bringing them home safely is my job, too. And I'm glad to have someone like you helping me."

A warmth spread through her. He looked serious. But—

"But you didn't want me around and only gave in because I did something helpful."

He gave a brief laugh. "That's the point, isn't it? Something helpful could grow into more. Or that's what I'm counting on. Do more of it!" He chuckled again.

"Count on it," she said, hoping she was capable of doing what she had just promised.

"And in case you're concerned, I understand that the stakeout you described involves sleeping outdoors for possibly several nights, camping out. I'm sure you understand that, too. But…well, if it makes you uncomfortable being alone with me that way, feel free to back out anytime and go home."

"Same goes for you," she said, liking his attitude… kind of. He wasn't meeting her eyes, as if he was embarrassed. But being alone with this man, sleeping alone with him out in the open…well, yeah, it made her uncomfortable, mostly with her own feelings. Damn if she didn't find this dedicated, uniformed sheriff's deputy too appealing. Too sexy.

But she wouldn't act on it, and wouldn't allow him to, either.

And, in fact, she reminded herself—as if she needed to—she had good reason not to become attracted to him or any other man. Not now, certainly. Not so soon.

And definitely not until she got to know someone

well enough to feel sure he wasn't just playing games with this "country girl."

"If I get too suggestive with you," she continued, still trying to keep the conversation light, "or you become uncomfortable for any other reason, well, I'll keep looking for my cows and you can go home."

He laughed. "Sounds like a challenge to me. Who'll get most uncomfortable first?"

"Not me," Melody lied, already feeling as if, despite everything, she'd have to work hard to control her own attraction to this man.

Casey wished just then that he could read minds. That way he would learn what Melody was thinking.

The idea of their sleeping out in the pasture together didn't seem to bother her. She'd sounded quite professional. She probably didn't feel the attraction he felt toward her, which was a good thing.

As they walked quickly, her expressions changed from light and humorous, to dark and apparently introspective and sad, and he was intrigued.

But he never asked her to explain. Figured she wouldn't answer, anyway. And now, he and the lithe, lovely ranch hand had reached the main house. The single-story, deep red structure had rich-looking wood and a beige roof.

Right now, his work vehicle, a black sedan with Sur County Sheriff's Department on the front doors and a light on top, was parked out front.

Beside it was a black luxury sedan. Clarence's? Casey asked Melody. "Yes, that's his." Melody looked down at the watch on her wrist. "He usually doesn't come home until around seven, but it's only five. I wonder if he's heard anything or—"

Before she finished, the front door to the house opened and the selectman stepped onto the porch. "Hey, you two. You're back. Did you find my cattle?" He had changed from the suit Casey had seen him in earlier into a long-sleeved charcoal T-shirt with the OverHerd Ranch logo in white. He clumped down the steps in his boots. Dressed this way, he looked a lot more rustic and older than Casey was used to seeing him. He still appeared relatively slender, but the skin at the corners of his eyes sagged and lines on his forehead were appropriate for his age...or was it stress that caused them to stand out?

"Not yet, sir," Casey said as the man reached them and faced them on the paved driveway. "But—"

"Then why are you here?" Edison demanded. "Why aren't you—?"

"I began showing Deputy Colton around, sir, and we went out to the fence," Melody said. "Since we didn't see anything helpful except for how the fence was destroyed in that area, we decided to come back for the night and leave early in the morning on a stakeout of the entire ranch and beyond, if necessary, on horseback. We won't return then till we find the missing cattle."

"'We'?" Clarence demanded, glaring at Melody.

Odd that, after wondering the same thing, Casey now felt he had to defend Melody and the fact he had decided not to protest any longer. He understood her rationale. And her presence might cost him time, since he would have to protect her above all else. But she was the ranch owner's employee. She had the kind of knowledge that could help him, as she'd mentioned. What she was doing could definitely be of assistance.

He noticed she didn't mention the charm she had found. Well, it might not mean anything, anyway. But he'd take care of checking into it.

"Ms. Hayworth was kind enough to offer to come along," Casey said. "We're going on horseback, and I'm sure, with her experience, she's a lot better rider than I am. Plus, she knows your land better than I do. I hope you'll allow her to come, sir. I think it will be to your advantage."

The selectman's expression changed from hard and angry to...well, resolved—and perhaps inquisitive. "And to yours, too, maybe, Deputy."

Casey saw the shock appear on Melody's face, even as he felt himself flush slightly. Had the selectman intended to be suggestive? Maybe not, but just in case, Casey said, "I intend to do my job and do it well, and I appreciate any assistance with it." He hoped he sounded strictly professional.

"Well, okay," Clarence said. "Hopefully that'll work. And I like what you said, Melody. You won't come back until you find my cattle. Right?"

"That's right." Melody looked relieved as she nodded vehemently.

"Right," Casey echoed. "So now I'll head back to town and return here early in the morning, around six thirty, okay?" He aimed his gaze at Melody.

But Clarence was the one to answer. "No, stay here

tonight. We've got some apartments available in our bunkhouse, where our hands stay. And they're fairly nice, right, Melody? "

"Absolutely, Clarence," she responded, which made Casey tilt his head slightly in confusion. She'd called him "sir" before, and now she was using his name.

Informality might be in order at the moment.

"I appreciate your invitation to stay here," Casey said to Clarence, "but I do need to go home. I'll need to bring the right clothing to wear on our stakeout, for one thing." And other appropriate things, as well, particularly since he didn't know how long they'd be out there.

"I get it," Clarence grumbled.

Good. But if Casey could have stayed, he would have; maybe he would have met more of the ranch hands. Gained more of their input about what had happened. But that wasn't in the cards right now.

He thanked the ranch owner and again said he'd be back bright and early the next day.

But Clarence wasn't buying that. "Nope, that's not happening. You can go home, get what you need and come on back as fast as you can—now. You're going to have dinner with Melody and me right here, just the three of us so we can talk, and then you'll stay here for the night."

The way he spoke allowed for no argument, but that was okay with Casey. He decided he liked this idea, since they'd be able to get an earlier start in the morning. He assumed that was also why Clarence was so insistent about his staying here overnight. Still, there were a couple of things he'd need to handle first.

"I'm still on duty," he told the older man. "And this is part of an assignment. I need to check with the sheriff first." Which he'd intended to do, anyway, although he had no doubt Jeremy would approve this intense way of tackling his investigation.

Staying at the ranch added another level to it, but that was likely to be all right, as well.

Especially if Casey—and Melody—actually found the cattle and the people who'd taken them.

But to do the stakeout as now planned, Casey would also need to pick up the camping gear he had at his home as well as some more supplies at a local store.

When he mentioned that, Clarence put up a hand and moved it as if he was erasing what Casey said. "No need. We've got it all here. You'll get it together tonight, Melody, right?"

"Of course," she said.

But Casey remained adamant that he needed to get some things. And so, a few minutes later, he found himself in his car driving along the rural ranch-surrounded roads toward town as the sky began to turn dark. There were a few other cars that were heading in the opposite direction, but no one was heading to town, like him.

He used the Bluetooth to call the sheriff. "Yeah, Casey?" Jeremy answered. "Did you find those missing cattle? And whoever stole them?"

"Not yet, for either of them." But Casey explained the situation to his superior officer, and how he was going to go on a stakeout with one of the ranch hands the next day.

"Would that ranch hand happen to be Melody Hayworth?" Casey could hear the suggestive tone in his boss's voice.

What was it with guys? Casey thought. Did they not believe in his professionalism?

Or did they find Melody as attractive as he did, and therefore let their imaginations run wild—their jealous imaginations?

Maybe he would change his mind and give it a try...

No. He was a professional. And clearly Melody was, too.

"It is Melody," Casey said in as formal a tone as he could muster. "She's good with horses, and she knows the ranch." Great reasons, even though talking about them was feeling a bit stale to Casey right now. "But looking for the cattle and the thieves—that's all we're up to. And I'll keep you informed."

But he realized as he hung up that he'd need to make a stop at the department to have one of the evidence guys check the charm for prints or origin, in case it could help lead to the perpetrator.

And there was something scratching at the back of his mind about it—but that was probably just because he hoped it would lead to something.

He still had a little ways to go before reaching the discount store he was heading to first, so he made another call, this time to Everett, who worked for the FBI in Phoenix. Everett was older by a couple of minutes, and they didn't look much alike. And for twins, their personalities weren't much the same, though they'd both gone into law enforcement.

"Hey, bro, what's up?" Everett said as he answered.

"On an interesting case," Casey replied, then described the cattle rustling and how he was attempting to find the missing animals and solve the situation.

He didn't mention that the ranch hand helping him was a woman, though. He'd never hear the end of it from Everett.

"I'll be out on a stakeout for as long as it takes," he informed his brother. "The ranch's owner has things set up so I should have power for my phone, but I haven't tried that yet."

"Well, better call the folks before you go, to let them know what you're up to in case you become unreachable."

Which Casey did next. He'd reached the store's parking lot, so he sat there as he talked to their parents, who both got on the phone.

Neither of them was in law enforcement. Dr. Ryker Colton, their dad, was an oncologist in town, and their mom, Maribelle Colton, ran the Cactus Creek post office.

As he finished and told them he was probably—but not absolutely—going to be reachable over the next few days, his father said in his aging scratchy voice, "Now, you be careful, son. Got it?"

"Got it, Dad."

"That won't keep you from coming for Thanksgiving dinner, or Christmas dinner?" his mom asked, her tone a sweet chirp, as always. "You know we'll want you to come. And...well, if you'd like to bring someone for Christmas, that's fine."

"Thanks, Mom," he said. "There shouldn't be any

problem with my being there for either one." After all, Thanksgiving was a couple of weeks away, and Christmas even farther away. "And if I think of anyone to invite, I'll let you know." His mind had flown immediately to Melody, of course. But he didn't know if she had family here, or friends she'd want to spend the holiday with.

Besides, under these circumstances…well, he'd just have to see.

Chapter 4

Melody wasn't sure what she'd expected dinner to be like with just the three of them—herself, Clarence and Casey—that night, so she wasn't surprised. But this felt unique.

And worrisome.

What if Casey and she didn't find the cattle and the people who'd stolen them? What if the stock weren't returned, especially after she'd sort of been singled out like this to help handle the situation?

They sat in Clarence's posh dining room, with its antique wooden table and chairs, a tall, matching buffet against the wall and a glimmering chandelier hanging over the table. Melody felt she should have worn something dressier, but the men with her also wore casual clothing. When Casey had gone home to grab what he'd need while camping out, he had changed into jeans and a deep blue long-sleeved T-shirt that hugged his chest—and he looked hunky in it. She had to make sure she didn't stare.

He was likely to wear that and similar clothes on their stakeout, although he'd need to keep at least his ID with him to show he was a deputy if—and when—they found the rustlers. Probably his gun, too. She would stay as remote as appropriate from him mentally, even though they would be physically near each other.

The large room was filled with the aroma of what was being cooked next door in the kitchen. Melody suspected she hadn't met everyone who worked here even now, after six months. Did Clarence have a special cook? Or was the person who prepared their food the same housekeeper who served it?

The housekeeper—Grace—was also dressed casually, in a long-sleeved black OverHerd Ranch T-shirt and jeans. She acted utterly friendly as she provided them each with a salad, a side of cheesy potatoes and, of course, a delicious steak. What else, at an Angus cattle ranch?

Melody had never dined in the main house before, had hardly spent any time here. There was a small kitchen and dining area in the bunkhouse where she lived and had numerous meals with her fellow ranch hands. That had seemed quite adequate since she'd begun working here. Clarence had always seemed nice enough, but she'd never felt close to her boss—nor should she.

"So how long have you been with the Sur County

Sheriff's Department?" Clarence had started to quiz Casey from the moment they'd sat down.

"Five years," he said. "It's a good place to work. The sheriff's good at what he does, and—"

"Yeah, I know that. I help him keep his job."

Melody felt herself blink, though not in surprise. Was that true? Or was it only Clarence's ego speaking? He had a big one.

"That's nice of you." She could hear the irony in Casey's voice and decided to change the subject.

"Clarence," she began, "you know we're going to start out early tomorrow. If there's anything you especially want us to do to find the missing cattle, we'd love to hear your suggestions."

"You'll be using the GPS, I trust."

She nodded, aiming a brief glance toward Casey, who looked amused somehow. "Yes. I've got the app on my phone like all the ranch hands, though I didn't use it when Deputy Colton and I were out there by the damaged fence. We did see a lot of hoofprints that indicated the direction the cattle had gone, so that's where we'll start out tomorrow."

"How about you, Casey?" Clarence asked. "Do you have the app on your phone? I made sure signals are available way out in all my pastures so cell phones work out there."

"I don't have the app," he said. "But I'd be happy to download it before we go."

"Right," Clarence said.

When Melody again glanced toward Casey, the deputy was looking at her, his expressive blue eyes making it clear he wanted to get out of there.

"Are you about finished with dinner?" the deputy asked as he glanced down at her nearly empty plate.

"I certainly am," she replied. "Because we need to get up early—really early, since I'll want to have a little time to make sure the horse we choose for you is the right one. I think we should head..." She hesitated for a moment, because she'd been planning on saying "head to bed," but that could sound suggestive. "Head to our rooms in the bunkhouse right away."

"Then I'll say good-night now," Clarence said. "Thanks to both of you, and keep me informed of your progress tomorrow."

It was six o'clock in the morning. Casey had awakened a while ago, showered, dressed and taken the things he had brought for their camping-and-stakeout expedition out to the bunkhouse lobby.

When they had arrived there last night, Melody had shown him to a small apartment on the second floor and given him a key. She'd let him know that her room was on the same floor but down the hall. He had gone out to his car—his own SUV—to retrieve the items he planned to take along.

When he'd come back in, he'd seen a couple of the guys including Pierce, whom he'd met before, and another fellow named Roger. They'd confirmed that the additional ranch hands had remained camping out in the pastures with the other cattle. Both of them indicated they'd be out in the pastures today, too. But Pierce seemed a bit displeased, hinting at his own desire to get out there and find the missing cattle. Casey thanked him but said that wasn't a great idea—particularly since he, a deputy sheriff, would be out there working on the situation, with help from another ranch hand. Pierce had agreed that was the better scenario.

Maybe Pierce and Roger had already headed out this morning, since neither appeared when Casey brought out his things and waited for Melody, who'd apparently already been there. His equipment, which he'd packed in the burlap bags some of the stuff had come in, wasn't the only camping gear in the lobby. There were a couple of substantial-sized saddle packs right by the front door that he assumed were Melody's.

But where was she? Should he text her? Call her? Maybe he should go to the kitchen to see what he could grab for breakfast, or maybe that's what she was doing. He'd be happy to see her again before they headed out.

He'd be happy to be with her then, too—which concerned him. He shouldn't have to remind himself to remain professional.

He started down the first-floor hallway in the direction he believed the kitchen was located and saw Melody emerge from a door at the end, her hands full.

"Good morning," she called, not muffling her voice at all. He figured no one else was there. She would be the one to know it.

She strode down the hallway and entered the lobby. Her black hair was once again pulled back into a ponytail, although she'd worn it somewhat looser last night at dinner. She again wore a blue denim work shirt and jeans, though her shirt this time was darker in color and unbuttoned part-way down the front to show a navy T-shirt below.

She looked damn pretty in it, despite how casual this outfit was, too.

He suspected she would look damn pretty in any outfit. Or none at all…

He immediately tamped down that thought. *Be professional*, he again reminded himself.

"I've got some stuff here for us to eat," she told him as she reached him. "Croissants and jelly. We can go wolf it down now with some coffee, if you'd like, before we go visit the horses. But we'll need to be fast."

"Sounds good. Is it okay to leave this stuff here?" He pointed to the small pile he had placed on the floor.

"It's fine. We'll be back soon."

Which they were. Their breakfast, unaccompanied by other ranch hands, took only about ten minutes.

He considered the kinds of food they'd eat out on the trail and figured she must have some items in her saddlebags.

Him? He'd picked up some dried fruit and beef jerky and energy bars—nothing that would go bad, and it could all be carried fairly easily.

Who knew how long they would be out in the pastures hunting cattle and people?

When they were finished, Melody helped Casey to download the GPS app onto his phone. She then told him to follow her to the stable. She picked up her saddlebags before he could grab them and she didn't seem inclined to allow him to be a gentleman and carry them along with his own stuff. She tossed him a slightly ir-

ritated look, which told him that any old-fashioned eti-
quette wouldn't be welcome around her.

He hid his smile. He liked that about her.

He was liking too many things about her.

For now, he closed the bunkhouse door behind him
and followed her along the paved pathway across this
part of the ranch behind the main house.

Melody opened the stable door fairly easily, it appeared, despite how full her arms were. Once inside, she
placed her saddlebags down on the hay-covered ground
and closed the door again behind Casey.

There were seven horses in separate stalls, though a
few stalls were empty and he figured that was because
of the ranch hands who had ridden off to the pastures
to protect the remaining cattle.

"We need to do this scientifically," Melody said,
standing beside him. There was a humorous catch to
her voice. "Let's start with this. Have you ever ridden
a horse before?"

"Well, yes, sort of." Smiling wryly down at her, he
described the few times he had ridden at commercial
riding areas in parks, and at family friends' farms as a
child, along with his brother, and also occasionally at
county fairs and the like. "No real riding on trails out
in the countryside, though."

"Got it. And I also know who's best for you. Witchy's
the horse here who's the least challenge to newbie riders." She led him over to a red-and-white horse a few
stalls down.

"Really? A horse named Witchy is fairly tame?"

"Yes. We'll try her. Me, I'll take my favorite—Cal."

She looked back toward Casey and grinned at him in a way that made him anticipate what she'd say next. "That's short for Calamity."

Casey couldn't help it. He laughed. "Sounds like we're headed for some wild riding. Witchy and Calamity."

"You got it," Melody said. "Now, let me get them saddled up and we'll try them out in the paddock outside. I'll also show you a bit of grooming and other things you'll need to know when we're out on the trail. Still, if all goes as I anticipate, we should be good to start our expedition in twenty minutes."

"You're doing great!" Melody called to Casey a few minutes later, meaning it.

She was seated on top of Cal, a sleek brown quarter horse and her favorite mount, while watching Casey trot around the perimeter of the corral on top of Witchy, a gentle and friendly pinto. The deputy sat tall in the saddle and appeared perfectly at home as he gently pulled the reins now and then to get Witchy to turn around and head in the other direction.

He'd seemed to have gotten the hang of it from the moment he had put his left foot into the stirrup and lifted himself into the saddle. Witchy's head had turned just a bit to see who her rider would be. The mare seemed fine with it, and Melody had only given Casey a few cues about how to remain seated comfortably and maneuver the reins to direct the mare.

She also told Casey how to gently squeeze with his heels to tell Witchy to speed up, and showed him how to click a bit with his tongue if he wanted her to go even faster.

As always, Melody appreciated being outdoors, listening to the clomping of hoofbeats at different speeds on the hard corral turf. She smiled, closing her eyes for a moment as she lifted her chin toward the sky. She felt alive here, and free.

This part, at least, was fun. And when she opened her eyes she saw that Casey had slowed Witchy down and was staring at her…and smiling, too. She looked down and shook her head, and directed Cal, with her heels, to start walking.

After a short while, Melody asked Cal to begin trotting as she directed him to get in front of Witchy. Then she urged him even further, and Cal began galloping around the corral, his mane blowing as he moved.

Melody glanced behind her. Yes, Witchy and Casey were keeping up. Not surprising, but it confirmed what she was thinking: it was time for them to head off to that critical pasture.

Chapter 5

They had almost returned to the site of the mutilated fence. It had taken much less time today, thanks to the horses and their speedier gaits.

Casey was happy to be on horseback. He liked Witchy and felt he was doing an okay job playing cowboy, as he rode this calm, obedient and enjoyable steed along the uneven, mostly grassy terrain.

Even more, he was enjoying watching his companion on this ride, Melody, on her somewhat more energetic equine, Cal.

She seemed more at home here, somehow, intensely watching their surroundings and handling her reins, gently guiding her mount in the direction she wanted. She wore a cap now, a blue denim one that matched her shirt, a lighter color than her jeans. He, too, wore a cap,

with his sheriff's department logo on it—the only current indication of his status as a deputy. But he needed
the shading of his face from the sun, which was bound
to become even more intense as the day grew later.

It was still early in the morning, around nine, and the
air was clear and a bit cool for Arizona, not surprising in
November. An airplane flew high overhead in the blue
sky, and Casey wondered for a moment which airport
it had come from and where it was going. It appeared
to be flying north, so maybe it had just taken off from
Tucson International.

Reflexively, as he'd done often during this ride, he
glanced behind himself at one of the two very large, but
not particularly heavy, saddlebags Melody and he had
filled. The other was attached to her saddle, similarly
behind her. With her instruction, they'd fastened them
on their mounts before leaving the stable. His contained
a small tent in case they had to sleep outside for a night
or two, which wasn't beyond the realm of possibility.
Each of them also contained lightweight, closely folded
sleeping bags.

The most bulky and necessary items they'd included
were water bottles, although Melody had assured him
that she knew where some creeks—perhaps including the one the town of Cactus Creek had been named
for—were located. They could utilize these creeks for
water, which they could purify with her portable water
filter. That way, they should be able to keep their own
water bottles filled, as well as making sure the horses
had drinkable water.

And possibly the most important thing? His duty belt

was hidden inside that saddlebag. It contained items he hoped he wouldn't need, but would be crucial if he did, including his gun. He'd also stuck his wallet and badge inside in case he needed money or to identify himself, though he kept his phone in his pocket since he figured he might need it quicker than the rest.

He'd fortunately had time to take that charm Melody had found to the sheriff's department to examine it and determine its likely source, as well as check it for fingerprints. They'd be passing the area where she found it soon, which he thought about now. If it turned out that the charm belonged to one of the perpetrators, it might be useful as evidence, but that remained to be determined.

And something about the charm was still tugging at his mind, though he remained unsure why.

"How are you doing?" Melody's voice came from beside him. She looked great on that horse, sitting tall, the reins held in her right hand, her jeans-clad legs hugging Cal's sides and her black boots in the stirrups. Her ponytail waved beneath her cap in the breeze as they moved forward.

Of course, Casey recognized that she looked great when not on horseback, too.

And despite knowing full well and even vocalizing that they were both there on business and would remain professional, he knew he'd have to be careful if they spent nights out here together to keep it that way.

"I'm fine," he said. "Wish I'd learned to ride a horse this way before."

"So you're having fun." Her words were a statement, and her smile was one of the biggest Casey had ever seen.

One of the prettiest, too.

Okay, he told himself sternly. *You like this woman. You like her appearance—and more. But keep it all to yourself.*

"Yeah," he responded. "Definitely fun."

"So here we are," Melody said as they arrived at the fence. "Our starting point, sort of. We'll head in the direction those hoofprints lead us."

"Let's check the GPS app."

Just before they'd headed out to the pasture, she had helped Casey download the GPS app, then shown him what the GPS portion of the tags attached to the cattle had looked like on her phone's map—a group of small, overlaid dots in one location. But without streets or even an indication as to what part of the open land the dots were located in, other than a rough idea of the terrain if the right part of the app was on, it didn't seem to Casey as if the GPS would be of much help except maybe to provide a general direction. But as with a lot around here, Melody was much more experienced and skilled in such things than he. He'd looked on his own phone and found the map, too.

"Good idea," she responded. "Let's do it before we head any further."

She'd apparently put her phone in her pocket, too, and pulled it out now. As she did, something else fell from her pocket—her wallet.

"Damn." She started to dismount.

"Here, let me," Casey said. "I'll pick it up while you check the GPS."

"Thanks." She nodded at him. "That'll save us a small bit of time. I assume you're skilled enough now to get on and off Witchy without my guidance."

"I assume so, too." He pulled his right foot from the stirrup, then lifted his right leg to move it around to the same side of the horse as his left one. Mounting and dismounting hadn't been that hard to start with, but he did feel as if the little bit of practice he'd been getting made him somewhat of a pro, like Melody.

Her wallet was in some grass just off to Cal's right side, and Melody's horse stomped a little as if he was uneasy to have Casey walking around. "It's okay." Casey stroked the brown quarter horse's side in front of Melody's leg, enjoying the feel of the soft coat. Cal seemed to quiet down immediately, and Casey bent to pick up the beige leather case.

As he did so, he noticed that the strap that normally held the two sides together was unsnapped, and before he could get it back together he saw Melody's driver's license inside. He barely glanced at it at first, but did a double take when he saw that it was a Texas license—the address wasn't in Cactus Creek, it was in Dallas. Understandable. Though she'd been here for six months, she must not have gotten herself a new one yet since moving here for this job.

But the more startling thing was…well, did this belong to this Melody? The picture was hers, and so was the first name, but the last name wasn't Hayworth, it was Ellison. Was she married? Using an alias for some reason? What was going on?

And how was he going to ask her?

He wouldn't. Not now. Whoever she was, and whatever her name, she clearly worked for OverHerd Ranch. The name situation was personal, since he'd no reason to suspect her of any crime—

None of his business, despite his curiosity.

"Here we are," he said brightly, holding out the now-fastened wallet to her.

"Thanks," she said. "And better get back up on Witchy. We're going to have a long day still, out here following the missing herd."

"Why? Are they on the move?"

"Looks that way," Melody affirmed. "And they're heading even farther from this area. The ranch is five hundred acres, a lot of it in that direction." She waved in front of them as he mounted Witchy once more. "But my suspicion is that those missing cattle are beyond that far end already or will get there soon."

Melody found herself looking away immediately as Casey handed back her wallet. Had he opened it? Was he that nosy?

Of course, it could have opened by itself when it fell from her pocket.

Maybe she should have shoved it into her saddlebag back at the stable, but she liked having a couple of things on her—her phone and her wallet.

She hadn't noticed whether he'd snooped into it or not, of course. She'd been studying the GPS map on her phone app, as much as she could, at least. The map sort of indicated major differences in the terrain such as deep ravines, moderate hills and high mountains, but not minor things like the usual rolling hillsides, waterways like streams, or any landmarks, although she wasn't aware of any out here. But it did provide the general direction of where the cattle were heading, and the distance of maybe fifteen or more miles from her current location with Casey.

Now she knew the cattle were farther away than they'd been, as well as the direction they'd gone, but whether Casey and she could follow directly would depend on that unfamiliar terrain. And if she was correct in her interpretation, they'd at least come to steep hills on the way that they'd navigate.

Melody now felt certain they would be spending at least this night out in a pasture on the way to catching up with the missing herd. She'd ridden out this way several times before since beginning work here, just to get the lay of the land, with one or more of the other hands with her. But she was far from knowledgeable with regard to the actual topography.

"I'm not really sure how difficult our route will be," she told Casey when he was back in the saddle and they were moving again. "Although the direction we're taking still looks right."

"Guess we'll just have to figure the rest out as it comes." His tone was somewhat curt, and she wondered why.

If he had been nosy enough to look in her wallet, he might have questions he wasn't asking aloud. Just as well. Since she had just finalized her divorce six months ago, her old Texas license still had her married name—Ellison. Thanks to the nasty, cheating jerk she'd been married to.

Which was dumb on her part, in many ways. She never should have married him in the first place. And once she had, she should have ended it faster. She'd had a sense sometimes that Travis was cheating on her, and it had hurt.

Well, at least being called a "country girl" had helped her make that final decision, and now she appreciated that, as a ranch hand here, she really was a country girl.

But one of the first things she should have done upon moving to Arizona was to at least get a new driver's license, so she'd never have to look at that old, unwanted name again.

At least Clarence had accepted her official divorce documents and hired her under her real name, which she'd returned to using, Melody Hayworth.

But she'd become so involved in her new job, so busy…well, that was her excuse, anyway.

And now, with this reminder, true or not, she knew she would do something about it soon.

Should she bring up the subject, explain it now to Casey?

No. If he'd been snooping, that was his problem. And she hadn't talked about her prior life much since she'd moved here, didn't necessarily want to do so now. Wanted to keep that difficult time behind her. She had definitely moved on.

If Casey asked about it, she'd answer. But right now,

he just seemed to be quiet and didn't interrogate her as a sheriff's deputy might.

Not that her prior ID should have made him suspicious of anything. She was a good, law-abiding citizen who was now trying to find whoever had stolen her employer's valuable cattle, get those cattle back to the ranch where she worked and then go about her usual life once more. She hadn't been involved in the theft, and to her knowledge no one had even considered the remote possibility that she was.

Except, perhaps, for Casey. He was a law-enforcement officer and he might have seen something that didn't quite fit with what he'd previously been told.

Whether or not that was the case, it now felt uncomfortable just riding beside Casey so quietly. They'd at least chatted before about the pasture and where the other cattle were currently ranging and what it was like to work on a ranch.

Working on a ranch. She had an idea how to start a potentially lighthearted conversation.

"Okay." She glanced over at Casey. His handsome face, which looked as if it had been chiseled from stone, was expressionless as he stared forward. Then he turned his head to look at her.

"'Okay' what?" he asked, still straight-faced.

"I like how you're now doing on horseback out here. Let's see how you do when we find the cattle. Of course, you're the law-enforcement guy and I know you'll need to take the thieves into custody."

"I intend to," he said, remaining solemn. "If there are a lot of them, I'll call for backup, assuming I get phone service out here as Clarence said we would, and if not we'll just follow carefully behind them until I can get a team to join us and arrest them."

"Right. But meantime, I'm now considering that you should have an alternate career. You're doing great riding. I'll have to see how you do with the cattle when we find them, but you look good up there, sitting on the horse and scouring the pasture with your gaze. I think you should consider becoming a ranch hand. Maybe even a cowboy yourself someday."

He pulled slightly on Witchy's reins, stopping her.

"You're kidding." He stared at Melody, and she stopped Cal. Casey's brown eyebrows arched even higher over his attractive blue eyes, a quizzical expression on his face—a good change from before, when he had no expression at all.

"Could be." She grinned widely at him. Then she attempted to grow more serious. "But what do you think of being here on the ranch? I mean, if you weren't trying to find stolen cattle, would you like riding here? Not just riding a horse, but riding one in this kind of environment? You don't necessarily have to herd cattle to be here, either."

"So you think I should become a ranch hand? You don't think I'm a good sheriff's deputy?"

She laughed and gently kicked Cal to get him moving again. Casey also gave Witchy a slight nudge so she started walking again, too.

Melody then looked at Casey. "I'm still sizing you up, Deputy. As far as I know, you're good at what you do. I think you'd be good at this, too. Could be that you can handle anything that life throws your way, right?"

"That's what I believe. In fact, I'm sure of it, but—"

"Great. I wanted to be sure that the man accompanying me on this potentially dangerous outing is smart and brave enough to handle it."

"I assumed you already thought so or we wouldn't be out here like this."

"As I said, I wanted to be sure." With that, she again gently kicked her horse and Cal's speed increased.

So did Witchy's, beside them.

Oh, yes, she'd already accepted that Casey was one good deputy, or his boss wouldn't have allowed him to be the one to take on this chase out here in the kind-of wilderness. To be the one to find the bad guys in this situation and either take them down himself—with her limited help—or get some colleagues to sneak in wherever they happened to be and help him out.

But all she'd wanted to do now was get them talking again. In a friendly manner.

Maybe also get him to reveal what was on his mind, although she believed she knew that part.

Why not just ask him? She might, if he continued to remain less friendly than he'd been before. It didn't make sense to be out here with someone who perhaps had some suspicions or concerns about her and didn't reveal them.

And…well, heck. She didn't really know much about him, either. Only that he was an officer of the law who'd been given this difficult assignment, including working with an unknown: her. She'd liked him before, and he'd seemed to like her.

And now? Well, who knew? But did she want to spend more time with this man out here without them getting along well?

Should she attempt to fix it by telling him all about her prior life?

Maybe so. But she wouldn't unless he asked.

Though she could find out more about him by asking some questions of her own—eventually.

But not now. Not until she could think this through.

What had that been all about? Casey wondered. Although he thought he might know.

She might have seen him peek into her wallet after all, even though she appeared to be engrossed in checking out the cattle GPS.

But why hadn't she just asked him?

Or should he have been the one to bring it up first?

Maybe so. And maybe he would bring it up sometime. For now, though...

Their horses were walking fairly fast, but the ground below them had started to become rougher, and he felt it in the way the saddle bumped his butt harder now as his horse's hooves hit the uneven surface. He pulled slightly on Witchy's reins. "Slow down, girl," he said, then looked ahead as Melody, on Cal, passed them. "Yeah, you, too," he called to his favorite—and somewhat difficult, at least right now—ranch hand. "Slow down." *And you, too. Call "whoa" on your attraction to Melody.*

Chapter 6

The warming Arizona day seemed to progress quickly as they continued to track the cattle.

They remained on horseback and though they were still in grassy pastures, they headed in the direction of some canyon areas filled with bushes and trees, which Melody considered a good thing. If they found the right spot, there might be some cover for where they'd ultimately sleep that night. And if she remembered correctly, there was also a small stream in that area, where they and the horses could get more to drink than they'd found earlier today, once it was filtered. Plus, she and Casey could also wash themselves.

They'd already come across other spots today where the terrain was irregular or the plant life was more vibrant—a good thing for when they needed breaks way out here in the middle of nowhere.

Melody had enjoyed the conversations they'd been holding; at her urging, they discussed things in their lives—some of the time, at least—that had brought them to where they were today.

"Do you like to see wildlife in the outdoors?" was one of the questions Melody asked Casey.

"I'm always after people who live a wild life," he said, making her laugh. "But if you mean do I like to see birds and animals and all out here, the answer is yes."

"Me, too," Melody told him, and they talked a while about visiting areas like this and various sanctuaries and zoos in their childhoods.

And Casey's enjoyment of animals upped him even farther in Melody's already climbing opinion of him.

Melody didn't bring up her divorce. She didn't even want to think about it.

Mostly, she peppered Casey with additional questions. Somewhat to her surprise, he didn't want to talk much about anything personal, either. His attitude might be forthcoming and professional, but he seemed almost shy as he responded in few words at first to her repeated questions about why he'd become a peace officer. Because he wanted to. Because it was a childhood dream. She considered that sweet. In fact, she was finding him *much* too sweet and appealing.

But that didn't keep her from pushing for more detailed answers when he attempted to change the subject. Besides, she was curious.

"Okay," he finally said. "It's no big deal, but if you really want to know…"

"I do."

"I grew up here in Cactus Creek," he told her, somewhat softly. He didn't meet her eyes as he spoke, and instead looked into the distance, as if viewing the area he spoke of. Maybe he was, in his head. "It's a great town, but like everywhere else there are good people and bad people. And I wanted to be out there helping to bring justice to my town. I got a degree in criminal justice from Arizona State and visited home as often as I could during the school years. I returned here full-time as quickly as I could and was hired as a deputy sheriff right away."

She had no doubt that he'd done well in school. He seemed highly intelligent as well as dedicated.

He was the right deputy to be out here with her on this assignment.

And he'd mentioned his twin brother. "Everett wanted to get into law enforcement, too, and he did, though a different way. He's with the FBI in Phoenix."

Was Casey close with his brother and the rest of his family? It certainly sounded that way as they talked. His parents lived in Cactus Creek, too, and it sounded as if Casey saw a lot of them. In fact, he was planning on spending the upcoming holidays with his family, and he said, "They're always happy to have guests join us at Christmas. Why don't you come, too?"

The idea had surprised, even shocked her. And made her feel all fuzzy inside.

For a minute. But then she began to have qualms.

"That's so nice of you. And your family. But…well, I might have other plans. Is it okay if I let you know?"

Any other plans would be simply to find a way to back out of this.

"Sure. Just give us a few days' notice if you're coming, and I'll let my folks know I invited you. I'll check with you again when the time gets closer."

"Sounds good," she said, feeling a bit relieved. He didn't sound upset or hurt. In fact, the invitation might just be a kindness to a near stranger, not because they were becoming friends.

He then turned around the conversation, pushing her to explain why she became a ranch hand.

"I come from Texas," she reminded him, as if that explained everything. And, in fact, it kind of did.

"I can tell," he said drily, which startled her. She glanced at him. She appreciated the Southern way of speaking, but her usual speech didn't include an accent. "Gotcha," said Casey as she looked at him quizzically. "Actually, I'm sort of surprised that you don't have more of a drawl. You sure you come from Texas?"

"Of course." She'd actually been born in New York State, but her parents had moved to Texas shortly thereafter. She'd learned to talk the way they did first and generally kept that up in her speech.

But just because her accent wasn't particularly Texan, that didn't mean the rest of her wasn't. She'd come to love ranching at a very early age, partly because her dad had become a ranch hand after they'd moved. Even when she was a child, she had loved accompanying him on horseback into the fields and pastures. He had taught her a lot.

Including how to love what he did for a living—enough that it was also what she decided to do.

Even these days, there weren't as many women who were ranch hands. But the owners of the place where her dad worked seemed to appreciate her take on watching and caring for their livestock, which also included mostly cattle and horses.

She told Casey all of this as they were riding, but not how she'd fallen for and become engaged to her high-school sweetheart, who'd convinced her to quit her job on the ranch outside Fort Worth and find another position in Dallas.

Then dumped her—and that hurt enough that she'd decided to leave the entire state of Texas, yet keep the career that she loved.

As much as their discussion reminded Melody of some of the bad things in her life, she realized she enjoyed talking to Casey about the good things from her past, especially because he seemed to enjoy hearing about them. Opening up to him about herself that way felt surprisingly wonderful.

She checked the GPS app on her phone now and then. Initially, the cattle kept moving but eventually stopped.

Of course, sunset was nearly upon this area. It didn't make sense for the rustlers to continue going forward in the dark. They apparently knew it and were likely settling down for the night.

And although Casey and she continued for a while,

it certainly wouldn't make sense for them to go on with no daylight at all.

So, as sunset grew closer, Melody had Casey join her while she investigated some of the land around them in search of shelter. There were, as she'd hoped, areas of greater vegetation.

And as darkness began settling around them, they settled down, too, in a spot both of them agreed would be a good one for the night, with a small stream nearby where they could collect water and use the filter on it.

There were even some pecan trees for cover for them and the horses—not that any rain was expected anytime soon, but there was less likelihood of being seen here, should any of the rustlers be snooping around to determine if they were being followed, than if they and their horses were on fully open ground.

Plus, they could tie the horses to a couple of the more barren bushes.

And camping out with Casey overnight? Melody wasn't sure how she should feel about that. The warmth at the idea that flooded her was highly inappropriate, but since nothing would happen anyway, she would just allow herself to enjoy it.

"How about you?" Melody asked Cal as she dismounted. "Are you ready to stop for the day?"

As if the horse understood, he made a snorting sound, looked down to the ground and nodded his head.

Melody had to laugh, and she heard Casey's deep laughter, too. "Let's see if Witchy feels the same way." Casey also dismounted, and though Witchy didn't ex-press how she felt, the mare didn't appear to want to continue on.

"Good. Let's assume this is our lodging for the night, shall we?" Not waiting for an answer from anyone, human or horse, Melody began to unhook the saddlebag from Cal's back. Casey came over to help, and they placed it on the ground that was covered with dry leaves. They did the same with Witchy's saddlebag. Then, also together, they removed each horse's saddle so they'd be more comfortable for the night.

Next, each walked their mount in a small circle, talking to them softly, just to settle them down. They removed the bits from the horses' mouths, though they left their headstalls on.

They soon collected water from a nearby creek, filtered it and carried it in metal containers to the horses.

Then, after returning to the spot where their saddlebags were, it was time to tie the horses' reins to the nearby bushes for the night.

Unlike the humans, the horses didn't have to wait for dinner. During the journey here, they'd been eating some of the grass in the pasture, which, of course, was of high quality. Melody liked the way her boss treated his livestock—and now she was happy there was good food out here for the horses, too.

Even so, as a healthy supplement, Melody also gave them some of the hay and grain she carried in the saddlebags.

And in actuality, the humans didn't have to wait for their dinner, either. This wasn't like a real camping trip, where they would light a fire and cook meats or anything else they had brought along. No, the dried jerky and fruits, as well as carrots and celery they had stuck in their saddlebags would have to do.

First, though, while there was still a small bit of fading daylight, they worked quickly together to raise the small tent. Melody was well aware that they hadn't had room to bring two. But, heck, they both were professional.

Although staying so close to Casey overnight…

She'd deal with it.

"You doing okay?" Casey asked her as she helped to stretch out the canvas and attach it to the small poles.

"Just fine," she said sweetly. "And you?" Surely he didn't think of her as some wimp—not out here. Not when she was the skilled ranch hand, not him.

"Absolutely." And he was the one to finish the unrolling and attaching. That was fine. She was using his masculine skills, that was all. And admiring them…

After they put the saddlebags inside and unrolled their sleeping bags, it was time to head down to the nearby creek again. Melody made certain to bring along some of the paper towels and sanitizer liquid she had packed so they could achieve some semblance of bathing without leaving chemicals in the water. Neither undressed completely, but they did unbutton shirts and pull up T-shirts and unfasten slacks, leaving underwear intact and also doing their ablutions with their backs to one another.

There. That wasn't too uncomfortable. At least Melody didn't think so.

And she avoided turning to peek at Casey's muscular physique while it was somewhat bared.

Or at least she didn't peek *much*. But she did manage to maneuver her own cleansing so she had to turn just a little here and there. And, heavens, this deputy sheriff really was one highly fit, highly toned—and extremely sexy—dude.

Was he doing the same with her? She managed not to look at his face.

If he was, she didn't want to know. Especially if he found her even a fraction as attractive as she found him.

Not when they were about to spend the night in such close quarters.

She was done with men, at least for now. She was still hurting some, even though her divorce had been six months ago. She no longer trusted most men. And she didn't have any interest in just having sex with one for fun.

Well, not much interest…and that was the problem.

Finally, both of them were done washing. Melody collected the few paper towels they'd used, then they walked back up the small slope together to the tent. There, they each said good-night to their horses. Casey opened the flap and Melody slipped inside first. Casey turned on the two small battery-operated lanterns so they wouldn't be totally in the dark.

"You ready to get your phone charged?" he asked after he pulled another battery-operated gadget from his backpack—yes, a phone charger.

"Sounds good, but I need to let people at the ranch know my progress first." Fortunately, the phone worked as she kneeled by the edge of the tent. There was, in fact, service out here, at least for now. Unfortunately, when she tried Clarence's personal line he didn't answer, so she left a message that Casey and she had made some progress but hadn't caught up with the herd.

She called the general line for the ranch hands next, hoping she'd get one of the senior hands, preferably Pierce, but instead one of her fellow newbies, Roger, was the one to answer. She gave him the same info as in the message to Clarence.

"Are most of the hands still out with the safe parts of the herd?" Melody asked.

"Yeah. I'm pretty much the only one around here tonight," Roger replied.

"So Pierce is out in the pastures, too?" Melody wondered which direction he'd gone, and which of the cattle he was helping to protect.

"Yeah. Don't know exactly where, though."

"Okay. Well, I'll keep in touch as much as I can." Not with Roger, though, unless he was the only one she could reach. And this way at least one person would be aware that she was still available by phone.

As she ended her call, she noticed that Casey was on his phone as well. He soon ended his call, too. "Just giving a status update to the sheriff, like you did with the ranch," he said. He'd obviously been eavesdropping, but that was fine. "So now is it okay to charge your phone?"

"One more thing," she said. "Let me check my GPS again first."

No difference in where the cattle appeared to be, judging by the multiple dots all in the same area as before. And they must have been on the move about the same speed during the day, since Casey and she didn't seem to be any closer.

As Casey connected their phones, Melody removed several of their meal items and two bottles of filtered water from their saddlebags, slipped his share to Casey, then sat down on top of her sleeping bag.

The ground felt solid beneath her butt, and she folded her legs to become as comfortable as she could. She noticed that Casey took a similar position.

Ah. Something else they had in common—among the few things she'd noticed, like attempting to save and return rustled cattle. And enjoying riding horses out in the wilderness while talking sometimes and staying quiet other times... Okay, maybe she was stretching things, since nothing she'd thought of was unusual. She didn't want to think about what else they might have in common—and hoped she wouldn't have to worry about finding out more that night when they attempted to go to sleep, *attempted* being the operative word.

But, no. She would go to sleep, or at least pretend to, without thinking—much—about the person across the tent from her.

For a while, neither of them spoke as they ate, though they did manage to glance at each other and smile a bit.

But Melody felt uncomfortable, knowing that their pseudo-meal wouldn't last long and they'd soon wind up just sitting there, or lying in their sleeping bags.

Would they talk? Stay silent? That remained to be seen. But talking would be okay, as long as it didn't lead to anything else.

"I like these fruit bars," Casey finally said, waving one of the items Melody had brought in the air. "I've had a lot of other kinds, of course, but there's something special about these."

"I like them, too," Melody said. "That's why I keep a supply at home and chose to bring them along on this trek." She went on to describe how she had found them online when searching for healthy and wholesome snacks. Good. This was a nice, safe subject for them to discuss.

They also talked about the pros and cons of bringing water with them. "Sure, there are quite a few creeks around," Casey said, "so I really like your portable filter. We don't have to carry many bottles this way. Once it's filtered, the water is clean enough to drink—but I don't particularly want to think about what else was in it before, what fish or bugs or whatever live there, what dirt it flows through or bacteria grows in it or—"

"Ah, but you definitely are thinking about it," Melody said with a laugh. This conversation didn't mean anything, but she felt happy they were talking, even if it was about nothing.

Although, seeing him in the shadows across the tent from her—even though he was currently fully dressed, as was she—she couldn't help thinking about how they'd been a while ago in that potentially nasty water that was okay to bathe in but not to drink without filtering.

Damn, but Casey had looked good only partially dressed.

"What about when you were a kid?" Melody asked,

to change the subject within her thoughts. "Did you ever go camping then? Drink the water?"

In the shadows, she saw him nod. "I did attend camps for a couple of weeks each summer when I was a kid. Even then, fifteen years ago or so, they were talking about some of the not-so-pleasant stuff that could be in the ponds or lakes or rivers we were near. In most cases, the camp counselors showed us how to boil what we'd drink."

Fifteen years ago, he'd been a kid going camping? Melody had figured he was in his late twenties, early thirties, so that worked.

But she… Well, for her to even think of dashing across the room and pulling off the guy's clothes— which, yes, the thought had crossed her mind—turned her into a cougar. Which would be fine with her. In fact, she rather liked the idea. But him?

Had he guessed their probable age difference? If he happened to feel any attraction to her, her being up-front about it could end any such thoughts on his part, depending on how he thought about such things.

But maybe it would be a good idea to mention it, partly to make sure any unwelcome thoughts on his part never fully materialized—and partly to make sure she wanted nothing to do with him, assuming he made it clear he had no interest in an older woman.

Although if age didn't matter… Or he did like older women…?

Well, it wouldn't hurt to find out. "I went camping a couple of times when I was a teenager, which was more than twenty years ago, not fifteen," she said. "When,

I gather, you were just a little kid too young to go to summer camps."

She watched his body stiffen just a bit in the scant light—or was she just imagining it?

"Interesting," he said. "How old are you? Me, I'm thirty."

Thirty. A ten-year age gap.

That could make a big difference as to whether they were attracted to one another.

Or at least whether he felt attracted to her, since his age was irrelevant to her.

"Oh, you're just a kid," she said with a hollow laugh. "I'm forty."

"Really?" He did sound surprised, which gave her an unwanted sense of pleasure. So did his following words. "You look so good and seem so physically fit—I thought you might be a little older than me, but not that much."

"Well, thanks," she said. "And now this old lady's going to lie down and, even though it's not especially late, try to fall asleep so I can wake up early in the morning and get on the trail again."

"Good idea," Casey said. "I'll do the same thing. Only—"

Before she could think about what he was up to, Casey had crawled the short distance between their sleeping bags and was suddenly right in front of her, on his knees.

He bent toward her, reached out and touched her arm, drawing her closer, then placed his hand behind her head. In moments, his mouth was on hers.

His kiss was hot, intense, amazing—and very short.

His lips explored hers, and he thrust his tongue into her mouth just a bit, only a hint of what other parts of them could do together...

It felt incredible, and it enticed her body to want a lot more.

He pulled away, though, looked down at her and grinned. "Hey, you kiss pretty well. Now with a bedtime kiss like that, I think I'll be able to sleep well. Good night, sweet senior citizen." He laughed, and in moments he was lying inside his sleeping bag with his back toward her.

Chapter 7

Now why had he done that? Because the lovely Melody, whatever her age, had appeared sad and somehow vulnerable, as if she expected him to say he'd never be attracted to someone that much older than him?

Or had he just been acting on that very unwanted attraction on his part? For, yes, she was clearly fit and smart and skilled at what she did, no matter how much older than him she was.

And after that kiss, despite its brevity and his attempt to be humorous, he knew he wanted her. Only for a night, or perhaps for several nights. He didn't want any relationship, though, especially not now. Not ever. It had nothing to do with their age difference and everything to do with the fact he'd been dumped by someone he'd thought he cared about and he never wanted to deal with anything like that again.

Dear Georgia. Leaving him at the altar like that, shattering his expectations for the future. Damn, but it had hurt.

Still, sex now with Melody? Oh, yes.

Not now, though. Not under these circumstances.

Now, he just lay there in the faint light of the lanterns, feeling the hardness of the ground beneath his sleeping bag digging into his shoulder and the rest of him, warmed maybe too much by the bag's enveloping cover…and the lust he was tamping down. Fast.

He listened to the silence across the tent from him.

He also listened for any sounds outside. He wasn't certain but thought he might have heard some clomps of hooves, just stomping down but not disappearing into the distance.

A snort, perhaps, also from a horse?

Nothing at all from Melody. What was she thinking? She surely couldn't have fallen asleep that fast.

Especially considering that kiss.

That kiss. Again, why had he done it?

And why had it seemed so appropriate, despite their being mere colleagues now, most likely for a while?

Yet, who was she really? He recalled again the name on her driver's license that he'd seen: Ellison, and not Hayworth. What did that mean? He was the one in law enforcement, and if he'd been in town he'd have attempted to check it out. Was she using an alias on this job? If so, why?

Or was she simply married without telling anyone about it?

And why did it make a difference to him?

But out here, Melody and he were the only humans in sight, for now just seeking stolen cattle. They might need to work even more closely together to get the cattle back and take down the thieves on their own, if there was insufficient time to bring in backup. He had to rely on her. On her integrity. And did an inconsistency in her name mean there were other inconsistencies in her life that he should be concerned about?

Or—

Well, despite the brevity of their acquaintanceship, the fact they were working together and the inappropriateness of any feeling for her other than as colleagues, he'd come to like the woman, in addition to wanting her.

She seemed nice. She liked animals. She had a job she liked and was dedicated to it and her employer.

Enough of this. He was overthinking the entire situation.

It was time to go to sleep. After all, they needed to awaken at dawn to continue their mission.

Sleep, he commanded himself.

And eventually, maybe an hour later, his body complied.

Melody woke up early, as she'd intended, the next morning.

Or maybe she hadn't slept at all. She thought she'd dropped off now and then but couldn't be certain. She hoped so, though. She needed to be wide-awake to continue their journey to find the missing cattle.

And falling asleep in the saddle was simply not an option.

She lay there for a short while, listening. Yes, she believed the soft, regular sound she was hearing was Casey's deep breathing, while he was still asleep. He wasn't snoring, though. That was a good thing.

She thought again, for maybe the millionth time, about his kiss last night. He'd been joking, right? Only it had turned her on even more than her attraction to him that she'd been fighting somewhat successfully—*somewhat* being the operative word.

And now?

Now she simply couldn't, wouldn't, let it happen again—no matter how much she yearned to be the one to start the next kiss…

Enough of this. It was time to get up. Get going.

For now, though, she remained as quiet as she could, as she unwrapped herself from her sleeping bag, slipped her shoes back on and glided out of the tent.

And stopped. It was gorgeous out here! She'd seen lovely Arizona sunrises before from around the ranch house, but this was spectacular. The sky was multiple shades of bright orange, a beautiful coverlet that lit up everywhere, showing the distant hillsides and mountains in silhouette. Some clouds in the sky gleamed white, streaking through the vivid color.

It was startling. Stunning. Incredible.

Okay, she had to share this. She hurried back inside and found Casey sitting up in his sleeping bag.

"You've got to come and see this!" she exclaimed.

Before she could explain what *this* was, he was on his feet. He was still dressed in the clothes he'd been wearing yesterday, as was she. This wasn't a place to stick on, or even carry, PJs. "Are the rustlers out there? Should I grab my gun?"

She laughed, but what did she expect from a deputy sheriff on the job?

"No, I want you to come see something good that has nothing to do with our cattle quest."

He looked puzzled. "What—?"

"Get your shoes on and I'll show you."

Like her, that was one thing he hadn't had on when ensconced in the sleeping bag. His boots, the same as he'd worn while in uniform, were beside him, and he immediately pulled them on.

Melody didn't wait any longer. She pushed open the tent flap once more, stooped down and straightened when she got outside.

It hadn't changed. That beautiful sunrise was still there. If anything it was even more breathtaking since the few white clouds interrupting the color had disappeared. The orange gleamed brighter, but Melody knew that it all could disappear fast as the sun rose even more.

"Wow," Casey said, stopping short. "I've seen great sunrises before, even out in open areas like this, but I've never seen any as amazing as this one." His tone sounded awed, even reverent, and Melody was surprised—no, shocked—when suddenly he reached out beside him and grabbed her hand.

His was somewhat cool and definitely strong as he

tightened his grip—not too tightly, but she had no doubt that he was there and hanging on, sharing with her, united in this special moment.

And her? She tightened her own hold as well. They were sharing a lot of experiences these days, and this one was definitely the most spectacular so far.

She found herself taking a step sideways, closer to him. Feeling his arm, in its long-sleeved blue T-shirt, against her own arm. Without thinking about it—much— she leaned her head against his arm as she continued to observe the universe around them, still holding Casey's hand for another minute. Longer.

Off to the side, she heard a couple of equine snorts, and that brought her back to her senses. So did the fact that the incredible orange of the sky had started to fade just a bit in some places to a softer peach.

"Wow," she echoed. "But I think it's time for us to start getting ready to go again."

"Yeah, you're right." He let go of her hand, and she looked up, smiling at him—and his eyes caught hers. He stared down at her, and she felt her face nearly freeze, then melt as his mouth moved downward and met hers.

This kiss was softer, more tender, than the one they'd shared before, but it still got to her. She reveled in the feel of his growing facial hair. She wrapped her arms around his neck and pressed herself against him there.

And felt regret when they both pulled away, as well as a bit of shock.

"I think we'd better stay away from sunrises," she gasped as she backed even farther away from him. "This one must have somehow mesmerized us." She

shook her head slightly, then turned to look beyond
Casey to the other side of their tent, where the horses
were still tethered to the bushes, stomping a bit as if demanding attention. "Let's get ready right now, and get
on our way." She said that even more firmly this time,
figuring he wouldn't object, anyway, but made it clear
she wouldn't tolerate an objection or delay.

Especially because her mind returned to reality. They
had a job to do. An important job. Finding and saving
those cattle. And who knew what kinds of danger that
might involve, even later today?

"Absolutely," Casey said, sounding all business, and
when she looked back she saw that his expression had
changed from the softer look he'd aimed at her after
their kiss to one that appeared much more serious. He
must be thinking about reality now, too.

Without looking back toward Casey, Melody hurried over to untie Cal's tether from the bush and started
leading him once more to the nearby creek, hearing the
crunching of dried leaves beneath her feet and Cal's
hooves in the cool morning air. She expected Casey to
follow, and he didn't disappoint her.

In fact, the guy seemed never to disappoint her in
anything since she'd met him—was it only a day or
so ago?

She would definitely have to be careful. When all
this was over, they'd have no reason even to stay in
touch, let alone camp out together and observe stunning sunrises.

And she knew only too well what it was like to have a
real relationship end with a horrible jolt. She didn't need

to let herself get so involved with Casey that she'd feel even a little upset when they stopped seeing each other.

They were business associates. *Period.*

For the next twenty minutes, Melody worked on ensuring that the horses, and their own gear, were ready to go.

After Casey and she performed some quick morning ablutions by the creek, they handed each other more of the snacks like those they'd eaten for dinner. She still had a bit of water left in her current bottle and added some water she filtered to refill it, then did the same for Casey and the horses.

Casey handed her back her phone after detaching it from the charger, which he returned to his saddlebag. She used that opportunity to check the GPS.

Damn. It appeared that the herd of cattle was on the move again. Most of them, anyway, increasing the distance from Casey and her, heading south. Was there something wrong with the system? One dot appeared still and not particularly near where the others had spent the night. Strange. But she'd had the GPS system act oddly at other times now and then.

Of course, she'd been able at those times to tell one of the more senior ranch hands, usually Pierce Tostig. He took her to a tech store in Cactus Creek and had her phone checked and, when it needed it, fixed.

That wasn't going to happen out here. She just hoped it continued to work adequately for them to locate the herd, even if it had occasional glitches. And they could always check Casey's phone, too.

"You ready?" she asked Casey, sticking her phone

into her pocket and mounting Cal. She studiously avoided casting a look toward her male companion with whom she'd shared such an amazing few moments earlier beneath the incomparable sky.

"Yep." Casey mounted Witchy as he spoke, then just sat there watching her, but only for a few seconds. "Let's go."

Which they did.

They were silent for a while. Melody couldn't help seeing that sunrise in her mind over and over—and reliving its aftermath somewhat.

Her hand enfolded in Casey's.

That kiss.

And her regrets about it. Sure, it had felt wonderful at the time, but she didn't want to feel that way about any man: *close*. She wanted to be with him. Wanted to touch him.

But that could lead to more touching…more feeling.

She felt a bit uncomfortable now and wanted to put those thoughts behind her and talk to Casey again like the professional colleagues they actually were and would continue to be, at least for a while.

He was the one to ultimately break the silence as the horses kept walking at a swift pace through the grass and along the irregular meadow turf in the cool November morning. "I assume we're headed the right way, according to your GPS, right?"

"Right," Melody agreed. "The cattle seem on the move toward the south, and that's the direction we're going. We need to speed up a bit since they're continuing to move at the same rate as before, and it would take us a full day to catch up with them if they were standing still. There might have been a glitch, too." She mentioned seeing the lone dot by itself. "Nothing major, fortunately. Even so, I just hope that's not the case now."

"I hope so, too."

They were both silent again for maybe a minute. Melody didn't like it. She looked at the vast green pasture in the direction they were heading. It was also broken up here and there by patches of trees or bushes and was a very pretty outdoor venue with a purpose: feeding grazing cattle.

And horses, since, as they weren't traveling extremely quickly, Cal and Witchy occasionally stopped to bite into a patch of grass, and she and Casey let them.

Getting to their destination a few minutes later would be fine if their mounts remained healthy and well-fed.

But— "What are we going to do if your GPS is entirely wrong?" Casey asked, aiming a troubled frown toward her. "Is that possible? I assume the one I downloaded would be the same."

"Yes, it would. And it's possible for the GPS to be wrong, but very unlikely, fortunately. I've talked to other ranch hands about that kind of possibility, and also the tech guy in downtown Cactus Creek who takes care of the ranch's system as well as the apps on our phones, and I never got the sense that there could be that kind of a major problem."

"But is the system obvious on the cattle? Are the rustlers likely to know about it and try to find a way to turn it off or, worse, somehow aim us in the wrong direction?"

"Again, yes, that's possible. But our Angus cows are all black, of course. Their tags that contain their ID numbers and GPS chips are dark and purposely attached to their ears, where they're not particularly visible to people, even those who are specifically looking for them. But even so…"

She had just remembered her own concerns about cattle security when she had started working at Over-Herd Ranch and had mentioned them to Clarence and the other hands.

Clarence had scoffed at her worries. He was the one in the business and he had done his research—or at least he'd hired and spent a lot of money for people who really knew what they were doing to install these kinds of location systems. Or supposedly knew.

Even so, she'd had a suggestion. "What about bringing on some herding dogs and a trainer or two?" she'd asked him. "There are several different breeds that are popular and apparently quite skilled. They can help to gather and keep track of the cattle and find them if any go missing."

"Yeah, right, I've considered that," Clarence had responded. "But that's an added expense and, worse, having dogs around sniffing and circling them and barking might only make the cattle nervous. Our cows need to be able to procreate without getting all anxious and edgy because there are dogs around giving them a hard time."

Melody had considered doing some research and providing Clarence with evidence that having herding dogs around would be a big plus rather than a problem, but she'd decided against it. Sure, she'd had a lot of those kinds of dogs around at the ranches she'd worked at in Texas, but right now she needed to be sure to keep *this* job.

And criticizing the ranch owner, who also happened to be a town bigwig, wasn't a great idea.

So she'd shut up about it.

And wondered now if she should have tried again.

She mentioned the idea to Casey. "Not that I'm an expert, but I've had good luck at past ranches where I worked, but Clarence wasn't interested in giving it a try."

"Too bad. I like the idea. And if there were dogs at OverHerd now we could have appropriated them to help us out here."

Melody felt a small surge of warmth inside that she quickly tamped down. He liked her idea. But so what? Clarence hadn't, and that had been what was important then.

And now?

Now it was just Casey and her—alone.

Chapter 8

The slightly cloudy sky was mostly blue now, though it was still fairly early in the morning. Casey was glad that Melody, who now rode quietly beside him, had awakened him for that amazing sunrise.

And had held his hand—well, let him hold hers—while they watched it. And shared a kiss…

Okay. He was overthinking this, as he tended to do about Melody. Sure, he enjoyed being with her. Sharing things like the sunrise…and their kiss. But so what?

He could admire her as a ranch hand, one who apparently felt comfortable instructing him in what he needed to know to survive and to do a good job out here chasing cattle and suspects. Even admire her looks. She appeared to be one heck of a woman.

That didn't mean he should allow his admiration for

her to get out of hand, not only now, but also as their assignment continued.

For now, he looked down at his horse's neck and mane. Witchy was a nice, calm girl who walked steadily enough to keep Casey comfortable on the hard saddle he'd put back on with Melody's help, along with the saddlebag. Today it had seemed pretty much routine. A stakeout with a beautiful cowgirl wasn't really something he'd imagined while thinking of his career with the sheriff's department, but it was enjoyable for now, partly thanks to Melody's tutelage.

When they actually found the missing cattle, things would change. He'd be in charge of handling that and making sure his department sent whatever backup was needed to bring down the perpetrators.

He recognized that he was thinking a lot as he rode this morning. Melody and he had been quiet for a while, after she'd described how she had suggested to her boss, Clarence, that having dogs around would help with herding and locating lost steer. He'd thought that was a good idea, too. Another thing to admire about her, and maybe to talk about as they continued riding along the turf in the direction where the main herd of cattle appeared to still be heading.

First, though, Casey did wonder about, and considered asking more about, the lone GPS dot Melody had shown him. A cow who'd wandered away from the herd, or a problem with the GPS? Melody didn't seem certain and, in fact, had mentioned some of the app's quirks—which could spell disaster if there was a glitch taking them in the wrong direction somehow.

But he was just speculating, worrying for nothing, hopefully. Time to ask those questions.

"I like how you suggested those dogs to Clarence," he began. "Not that I know much about ranching, but that sounded like a good addition for a ranch owner to help ensure that he always knows where his cattle are. And yes, I know it's not as technologically advanced to have a dog or two compared with a satellite-assisted GPS system, but it still sounds good and potentially useful. You said that you came from Texas and worked on a ranch there. Did they have dogs?"

"The first one did. That was partly because of my father's suggestions back then, and the owner liked the idea and started always keeping trained dogs to help."

Ah. He was getting some of her background. Interesting.

"So you began working at the same ranch your dad did? He was also a ranch hand?"

"That's right. He taught me a lot—and I liked it."

Then why had she moved here? he wondered. He wanted to ask, to learn everything, but if she'd left because her dad was no longer around, no longer alive, did he really want to remind her? That might be cruel and also might end any chance at a nice, friendly, neutral conversation as they continued.

Was she close to her family? Did she have siblings? Did she want to have kids someday herself?

Well, that wasn't going to be a topic of their conversation.

He began talking anyway. "I'll bet your father's re-

ally proud that you decided to follow in his footsteps."
He aimed a smile at her.

And now he did see some emotion written in her expression. But it didn't appear to be grief—only pride.

"Yeah, he was. Still is."

"Then why aren't you still working with him?" Casey
blurted. Maybe it wasn't his business, but he was curious nevertheless.

He watched as the emotion on Melody's face changed
to— What was it? If he had to guess, it was fury.

Wow. Maybe this wasn't a good idea, after all. But
his curiosity increased exponentially.

"This isn't something I like to talk about," she finally
said, hissing out the words between her teeth. "Or even
think about. But I quit working for the ranch where my
father was a few years ago. I married a guy I'd known
for a long time who wanted to move from Fort Worth
to Dallas, which we did. And then—"

"And then?" Casey repeated, encouraging her to continue when she stopped talking.

"And then I got a divorce and decided to leave."

No, Melody didn't want to think about her past, let
alone talk about it. But Casey seemed nice enough in
his attempt to make conversation and learn how she'd
wound up here, and the only way to prevent telling him
would be to lie or to shut up.

She didn't want to do either. And now she'd opened
the door to describe the rest of it.

She shook her head as she continued to look forward

and not toward her riding companion, concentrating for a moment on the feel of Cal walking beneath her.

Why had Casey decided to be so nosy? And now, her mind was back on her divorce, at least a bit. She had to think of something else.

At the moment, Casey seemed to be struggling to find something to say, and she almost smiled at that.

"Oh, sorry to hear that," he said finally.

Oh, what the heck. The subject had been broached.

She didn't want Casey's sympathy or anything else, but she could be frank about it, anyway, now that she was thinking about it, then make things clear, when she was done, that the subject was now off-limits.

She manipulated the thin, cool leather of the reins in her fingers without communicating any changes in direction to Cal, needing something else to do besides think of what she was talking about.

"Look, here's what happened. It doesn't hurt for you to know about it, and it doesn't hurt for me to talk about it." Not much, at least.

Thinking about it—how she'd been used, how she'd been insulted, then dumped—well, that still hurt.

She didn't mention Travis's name but figured she didn't have to. If nothing else, Casey might recognize that her married name was Ellison, presuming he had seen her driver's license as she believed.

Nor did she have to explain the horrible, hurtful details.

So she kept it light and somewhat brief, even though she knew she could have talked for hours about what a jerk Travis was.

"The guy I married I'd known from high school in Fort Worth. He was a smart guy, attended college, even got an MBA. Me? I was happy working alongside my dad as a ranch hand, but my then fiancé didn't seem to mind. In fact, we married soon after he got his degree. He'd told me by then he wanted to move to Dallas, which was okay with me. I even found a good job there. But…well, things only worked out for about two years. It was a mutual decision to divorce."

Yeah. Travis wanted to marry Loretta, whom he considered a "real woman." He had no interest any longer in the *unreal* woman, a mere "country girl."

And Melody didn't want to stay married to an SOB like him who insulted her over and over again. And also had an affair that he'd denied, of course—at first. Plus, if he didn't like being with a "country girl," why had he married a ranch hand in the first place?

Not that she'd made a lot of money, but Travis had seemed happy that she was out there doing something productive.

The thing was, after they were divorced, she just couldn't see heading back to Fort Worth in shame to work on the ranch with her dad again, around so many people who'd known Travis and her in school. Instead, she looked around and found the job here, in small but enjoyable Cactus Creek, Arizona.

But she didn't go into detail about it with Casey. She simply said, "Things just didn't work out between my ex and me, but I wasn't about to let my divorce get me down. I decided to use it as an opportunity to try something new, still doing what I loved but finding a new place to do it—right here."

"You sound as if you did the right thing," Casey said. She'd been looking straight ahead, then down at her hands again as she spoke, trying to keep her feelings to herself. But now she glanced at him and saw what appeared to be relief—and was that admiration, too?—on his face. "Exes can be hell, can't they? You one-upped me, though. I wasn't married, but mine dumped me at the altar four years ago."

"Really?" Melody said. "Wow. That sounds pretty bad, too. What happened?" Poor guy. That must have hurt.

Maybe she and Casey did have something else in common.

And they both were single now…

In any case, she now felt curious. Was what had happened to him as bad as what she'd experienced with that louse Travis? And did he finally feel ready to move on with another woman?

Okay, he didn't have to talk about being dumped. He definitely didn't want to think about it—although his thinking about it happened too often.

Like right now, partly thanks to Melody's story.

She was obviously emotionally stressed from having told him about her ex. And he needed to continue riding with her, working with her, conversing with her.

Maybe if he shared the most miserable part of his life with her, as she'd just done with him…

He'd just keep it short. And light. Or at least as light as possible.

"Well, the thing is," he began, "I met my ex, Georgia, and first became close to her, because her brother Sean was my twin's best friend when they were kids."

"So what happened?" Melody asked.

"Georgia never really explained except to say she'd made a mistake. I gathered from Everett that Sean hadn't been thrilled about our engagement. Didn't think I was good enough for his sister, and best I could tell he finally convinced her, when we were about to be married, that he was right."

"Did you ever talk to Sean about it? Did Everett?"

"Sean wouldn't talk to me," he said. Casey had tried, though. Wanted to know whether what he'd come to understand was true.

He had even tried talking to Sean's wife, Delilah, an accountant who seemed to be fairly levelheaded, to see what he could learn from her, but she'd avoided him, too.

And Georgia? She'd been pretty, though not as pretty as Melody—at least not the way he remembered her. She'd been closer to his age than Melody.

Not that it mattered. He'd been dating Georgia for a while before they got engaged and were nearly married. He'd loved her. A lot. Which had turned out to be a big mistake.

He had no romantic interest in Melody, so her age didn't matter.

But he had no intention, after what had gone on with

Georgia, in getting romantically involved with a woman anytime soon. Probably ever.

He'd seldom seen Georgia after she dumped him so nastily, which was probably a good thing. They'd both actually shown up for the ceremony, but she wasn't wearing her wedding gown. Instead, she told him then that she wasn't going through with it.

Her excuse? She had decided she didn't love him after all and had no interest in being married to a deputy sheriff.

He didn't even know what she did for a living now. She hadn't had a lot of ambition when they were together, so it was probably for the best that she'd dumped him, or maybe he'd have been their sole breadwinner.

He did have the impression, though, that Sean, too, wasn't wild about him partly because he was in law enforcement. That made Casey wonder if Sean had been interested in some kind of criminal activities—or maybe he'd already started back then.

Casey never tried to find out. None of the cases he'd dealt with had ever involved either Sean or Georgia, or even Delilah. Too bad, in a way. He'd have liked a bit of revenge for the misery he had gone through. Love? Yeah, he'd felt it. Too much.

But that was then. Now—well, it wasn't worth going through that hurt ever again.

"So how did you feel? How do you feel now?" Melody's tone sounded curious.

Really? They were going to have a longer conversation about it?

He should have hated the idea, but somehow, talking with someone he was now working with, someone he liked—and someone who'd suffered through something similar and could most likely understand if he snarled as he spoke about it more—didn't seem so bad.

He looked over at Melody to find her watching him. She seemed to be staring at him intensely—just as he'd done to her—in an attempt to read him.

"It was hard at first," he admitted, looking away to study the pasture in front of them as if he was concerned about where they were going. Which he was. He took a deep breath and continued. "I'd imagine you, if anyone, can identify with what it's like to have had expectations and hopes for the future—the long-term future—and believe that it'll be good, enhanced by a relationship that seems long-term. Forever, even. Fulfilling. Sharing dreams. And…heck, I must be sounding like some kind of oddball idealist. That's not me. But even so…"

He heard a small laugh and again glanced toward Melody. She was shaking her head a little, causing her pretty ponytail to sway back and forth. He felt his heart shrink. She didn't get it. She did consider him an optimistic weirdo or something. And—

"Oh, yes, I know what you're talking about," she said. "In fact— Well, with you, you might have had some wonderful hopes and wishes for the future. Me? I was already married, for more than a year, in fact, before I let myself recognize any problems in the relationship. And at first I imagined I was dreaming it. Maybe even having stupid thoughts of my own that this wasn't working and that I needed some new guy in my life already." She stopped for a moment, then blurted out,

"But I finally realized, when it was over, that I didn't. I didn't need the jerk I was married to, and I didn't need anyone. *Don't* need anyone else." She went silent for a moment. Casey glanced toward her briefly and saw she was staring at the back of Cal's head with an expression he couldn't read. "But it was still damn hard," she said.

"Yeah," Casey agreed. "It was still damn hard."

They rode along in silence for the next few minutes. Casey's mind kept mulling over what Melody had said, and how, though their circumstances were definitely different, they'd both suffered some pretty rough times thanks to relationships gone bad.

Really bad.

He had an odd desire to get off his horse and give Melody a hug in understanding, but that would be inappropriate.

Plus, it might give her the wrong idea. He'd definitely made it clear that he didn't want another relationship after what had happened before. Not now, certainly, and maybe not ever.

And he'd understood that Melody had the same opinion of getting too close to another person of the opposite sex.

Sex. That was not the same thing, even though romantic relationships usually led to it.

Did he want to sleep with Melody? He certainly wasn't against it, but it would definitely be a bad idea—even worse now after he'd learned they weren't just associates with the same assignment from their respective employers.

They were both smart individuals who'd learned a lot from what being with the wrong person could do to you.

So for now—

"I appreciate your understanding of that miserable mess," he finally said. "And I definitely understand that you went through something similar. We're comrades in arms in many ways." He laughed and was delighted to hear laughter from Melody, too. Somehow his recollections seemed to hurt a bit less now after he'd shared them. He was glad she'd shared hers, too.

"We definitely are," she said. "Empathy's the thing between us, for good reason." She hesitated, then went on. "But let's leave it alone now, okay?"

"Unless I think of a way we can each help the other get revenge," Casey said, keeping his face straight as he looked toward her yet again.

"Hey, I like that idea," Melody said, her expression thoughtful as she nodded her head up and down.

Then they both smiled at one another, and Casey felt the heat of attraction pulse through him even as he told himself that wasn't what this was about.

Camaraderie was.

"Okay," he finally said. "Let's think on it. Meanwhile, tell me if you're aware of anyplace it'd be good to stop for a while and grab our huge, delicious lunch."

More laughter. And that made him feel really good.

Chapter 9

Melody enjoyed their ride for the rest of the day. Not that she hadn't before, but they actually now seemed like friends. They'd each experienced a difficult aspect of life in different ways and survived, and shared it.

Would this new bond survive after they achieved their goals of locating the missing cattle and bringing down the thieves? That remained to be seen. But right now, she hoped so.

They continued to chat a lot as they rode forward, picking up the pace a bit. No more discussion of their horrible exes, at least not for now.

But they did see wildlife here and there, which made for some interesting conversation. There were lots of lizards out here, for one thing, and she was the one to win their contest of seeing and identifying the deadliest. She saw a Gila monster and pointed it out, and they were both very careful to guide their horses way off to the side. Gila monsters were dangerous and had some pretty nasty venom.

But reptiles weren't the only wildlife around. They saw more birds flying by. "They look like small hawks," Casey said, pointing at one that came relatively close.

"They're kestrels," Melody informed him.

Melody also pointed out some brown-headed cowbirds, which seemed appropriate for their quest—although she also mentioned they were a type of blackbird. They saw a few jackrabbits, a couple of different kinds of rodents that Melody believed were Arizona cotton rats and quite a few mice. There appeared to be more wildlife out here than they'd seen yesterday. Of course, they were a bit farther from civilization—assuming that the ranch house and related buildings were considered civilization.

Or maybe they were just paying more attention.

They turned it into a game. "Whoever sees the next animal out here gets to have first choice of which energy and fruit bars to have for dinner tonight," Melody announced at one point.

"Hey, that'll be me," Casey responded, his tone full of good humor, too.

As it turned out, Melody was the next one to see a creature. It was another kind of lizard, one not nearly as scary as the Gila monster. She didn't directly point it out to Casey, but she waved her arm generally in that direction.

"Hey, I see a lizard," Casey said, pointing directly toward where Melody had indicated.

"Oh, yeah," she said, pretending to be surprised. "Looks like it might be a fence lizard to me, though they don't really need fences to survive, fortunately."

"But you saw it first, right?" Casey sounded amused, and when she looked at him, he arched his brown eyebrows and cocked his head to the side.

"Who, me?" She smiled and batted her eyelashes, and his laughter seemed loud enough to scare that lizard—and it did run off, which caused Melody to chuckle, too.

"Maybe we should write down all we see," Casey suggested.

"Maybe so—especially if we start seeing any signs of cattle besides their hoofprints."

There were more grassy areas than dirt or mud where hoofprints would show up. But there were also areas where that greenery had been tamped down, most likely by cattle walking through it. That, even more than the GPS, told them in which direction to continue.

And so they kept going, with occasional breaks so they could walk around a little themselves, especially in areas with bushes around, and the horses could get a short breather without people on their backs.

They also discussed their pasts a bit more, though Melody was glad that neither of them brought up their exes or their respective breakups again.

Instead, she really had a question. "You mentioned that you have a twin, right?" she asked a short while after they'd seen and pointed out another rabbit. Cal walked right by it without paying attention, but the rabbit certainly noted their presence and leaped away.

"That's right—my brother, Everett. He was born only two minutes before me. That makes him my older brother, right? He certainly thinks so and has sometimes rubbed it in if he wants to get me irritated."

"That's silly," Melody said, unable to help herself as she stared toward the horizon, which was starting to take on some color. Soon it would be sunset. She began looking ahead of them for a place to stop for the night, even as her mind continued to swirl around what they'd been briefly discussing.

Two minutes? Why would that make a difference?

But as they continued forward, she enjoyed the amusement Casey imparted to her about how he and his brother had behaved in classes as kids, from elementary through high school. Sometimes they were in the same class and often not, but either way they enjoyed goading each other about it.

And sometimes they gave teachers or fellow classmates a hard time, pretending that they weren't twins or even brothers.

His description made her a bit envious. She'd always been close to her parents, but she had no siblings.

But she'd wanted to add to her family by having kids someday. Not going to happen now, though. Not while she had no interest in remarrying.

"We drove our parents nuts at times," Casey admitted. "Silly, of course, but it was fun. When we tried it in school we sometimes got called into the principals' offices so we tried to be somewhat cautious about where and when."

"I'll bet," Melody said, picturing such mischief in her mind. And she also imagined how annoyed she would feel if any twins tried that around her.

Yet working as a ranch hand, she'd seen plenty of bovine siblings around who looked similar, or even identical, that she needed to tell apart. Angus cattle, in fact, were generally all black in color and closely resembled each other; their personalities, too, were often similar.

The first cattle she'd dealt with, on the Fort Worth ranch and then in Dallas, were generally Hereford or Holstein, and though there were similarities they didn't necessarily look alike.

Good thing, thanks to Clarence and his rules, that the Angus cattle she now worked with had tags that contained their names and ID numbers, as well as GPS microchips.

Eventually, Melody started leading them off to the east despite their general need to continue mostly south, but she noticed some hillsides with more plant life that way and she hoped for another creek, too.

Which, after a bit of hunting, they found, along with another good place to tether the horses on a couple of trees before the hillside they chose sloped down to the creek.

They now had a hint of a routine. They both dismounted, and Melody was pleased to have Casey help remove the saddles and saddlebags once more before they both led their horses down the hill to get water to be filtered to provide them with a drink.

As they'd done yesterday, both Witchy and Cal had eaten grass and extra feed along their route. And after grooming and checking over the horses, they tied up the animals for the night. Then Melody helped Casey raise and secure the tent and they put their saddlebags inside.

After they conducted their bathing ritual, they called their respective bosses after Casey turned on the lanterns.

Melody, sitting on top of her sleeping bag, wasn't particularly pleased that the reception wasn't great where they were. She was happy, though, that she reached Clarence on the first ring this time.

"Sorry about that static," he grumbled. "I'll have to get one of my tech advisors to check it out tomorrow. So—have you located my missing cattle yet?"

"Unfortunately, no. They seem to be continuing to head farther away, according to the GPS. It may still take another day or two."

"Great." She heard the sarcasm dripping from her boss and winced, but what could she do? "Just so you know, I've had the hands who were watching the other herds lead them back closer to the ranch rather than fanning out the way they were. It's easier for them to help each other take care of the other herds that way."

"I'd imagine so," Melody agreed. She looked across the tent at Casey, who seemed to be talking animatedly to someone. Was he having a better time with the sheriff than she was with her employer? For his sake, she hoped so. But she also knew they'd all be a lot happier once they'd found and rescued the stolen animals.

She couldn't help noticing, in any case, that Casey

looked relaxed in his jeans and the sweatshirt he'd put on over his T-shirt. Very relaxed.

Very sexy, especially since they were here for the night, alone once more…

And Melody had to keep her mind on what was important. That included not becoming attracted to this man who also would have no interest, after what had happened to his love life, in getting involved with her, any more than she wanted a relationship with him.

"And…damn it all." Clarence was suddenly yelling into her ear, bringing back her focus. "One of the hands who's supposed to be back here helping out isn't around. I gather he told a couple of the others that he'd go out and find the missing cattle and report back. Never mind that you're already spending—and I hope not wasting—your time out there and you've got a deputy sheriff with you."

"That's right," Melody agreed, and wondered who the disobedient hand was. If she had to guess, it would be Pierce; he'd seemed particularly concerned and interested in the case, and like their boss he enjoyed being in charge.

"Well, if you happen to run into Pierce out there, tell him to get back here where he belongs. Unless, of course, he's actually located the cattle." So she'd guessed correctly.

"Of course, sir," Melody said, rolling her eyes but glad he couldn't see that. "And I'll report back to you again tomorrow, one way or the other, assuming I still have phone service."

"Good. You do that." Clarence ended the call.

Casey wasn't talking any more, either. "I just let the sheriff know we're still out here trying," he told her. "No news wasn't good news, though." He tried to make that sound like a quip, but he clearly wasn't happy.

"Same goes for me and our town selectman," Melody said with a sigh. "I think maybe it's time for us to grab something to eat."

"Yeah, maybe that'll make us feel better," Casey agreed, and they both dug into their saddlebags for food.

When they were done eating, Melody decided to go back outside to check on the horses. "It's colder outside than it's been since we started out," she said to Casey. "I want to be sure they're okay and not bothered by the increased chilliness."

"Good idea," Casey said, and stood to accompany her. She liked that about him. He was always there for her, willing to help. He even swept the tent's exit flap out of her way.

She needed to ignore that—despite the way his eyes caught hers for a moment, too. She made herself keep going.

The horses still stood where their reins were attached to nearby bushes, and they both appeared relaxed, even sleepy. They looked up when Casey and she approached and Witchy even nodded, but neither appeared to need any further attention.

"You're the expert," Casey said, "but they both look okay to me."

"Me, too." She patted both of them nevertheless and got some curious but apparently neutral looks from their mounts, who didn't attempt to move, at last not at that moment.

Suddenly, Casey grabbed her cold hand, tugging her along until they were back inside the tent. She was even more amused—maybe—when, after helping her to get down on her opened sleeping bag, he joined her there, sitting closely beside her with his arm around her.

Which felt good. Much too good. And not just because it helped to warm her a bit.

She was even more aware of him than usual. Of his body, touching hers. Not in any sexual way, and yet she couldn't help thinking about how his hip met hers, how his warm side also pressed against her, somehow turning her on. How his hand, which latched on to the outside of her leg to pull her closer as they sat there, increased her awareness of his fingers and where they might go if they moved, rather than simply holding her loosely.

And yet, she just sat there, as he did. They talked more about their respective pasts and what had brought them to this point in their lives.

Eventually, Melody felt herself relax as they continued their light conversation.

This was fine, she told herself. Two professional colleagues keeping each other comfortable.

That was all it was…right?

Keep talking, Casey told himself. That way, he could just hang out there with Melody snuggled beside him as he sat up.

Her light, feminine scent, maybe due to whatever she put on after their attempt at washing, intrigued him.

So did the feel of her. The sweet, humorous tone of her voice…

Plus, Casey enjoyed, maybe too much, her responses to his questions about what her dad had taught her—and not taught her—about being a ranch hand.

Her father had taught her to love animals, although that might have happened, anyway. To want to take care of them. To love the outdoors and work there to achieve everything necessary to ensure that the cattle, horses—and sometimes dogs—were well cared for and also worked well with each other.

Would she be as caring with a husband? Kids? Somehow Casey thought so. But he wouldn't be the one to find out, if anyone did—although the idea of her possibly being so loving? Well, it intrigued him.

He cast his thoughts aside.

"What was your favorite lesson?" Casey finally asked.

"When my dad showed me how to ride horseback and cull a cow from the herd without scaring either of them, or myself. And then he had me practice it. It was sort of the initial lesson of how to become the best ranch hand I could."

She'd moved even closer beside him, if that was possible, as she spoke. Even laid her head against his shoulder, moving it so she talked upward, toward his ear.

He wanted to pull her even closer, maybe on top of him.

Better if he was on top, though…

No. He had to keep his mind under as much control as his body. "Sounds great," he said. "Everett and I didn't become interested in law enforcement thanks to our parents, though. Our dad is a doctor, an oncologist, and he loves what he does, but neither Everett nor I ever aspired to become an MD. Our mom's the local postmistress. She's a great lady—didn't want us to follow in her footsteps but did want us to give back to our community. So, in our ways, we have—even though Everett's not living here now."

"Then I assume your mom's fond of Cactus Creek, too," Melody said.

"Yes, she's lived here all her life as well. But though our folks were nice and encouraging, they didn't particularly inspire us with how to spend our lives."

"So how did you choose law enforcement?" Melody asked. Her voice was starting to slow down and sound sleepy.

But Casey wanted to answer her question. "Well, somewhere along the line we heard of some distant relatives, more Coltons, who didn't live around here but were cops. Everett and I both became fascinated, looked into it more, watched long-distance, to the extent we could, what those relatives were doing…and here we are."

"Yes, here we are," Melody repeated, her tone soft.

"You sound tired," Casey told her. "Ready for some sleep?"

"Sure," she said.

He started to move away from her, to cross the small expanse of the tent to get to his own sleeping bag, but she grabbed his left hand until he turned back toward her.

"It'd keep us both warmer if we slept together," she said, and then her pretty eyes widened beneath the light of the lantern. "And I do mean *sleep* together," she clarified.

"I figured," he responded with a laugh. "Sounds good to me, as long as we actually get some sleep that way."

They were in Arizona, not Antarctica. But it was chilly, and staying warm would help them sleep to prepare for the next day.

Melody replied to his comment. "What, do you think staying that close will cause us to lose the professionalism we've been so good at so far?"

"I guess we can find out." He winked at her.

But in the next few minutes, they did lie down together, both of them on top of Melody's opened sleeping bag, with Casey's spread over them.

They started out lying side by side, and he gathered that Melody actually fell asleep that way.

Not him. Not at first.

He was too conscious of her presence.

Of her sexiness, even as they worked at being professional despite her being so close, pressed up against him just slightly, yet emphasizing how wonderful her nearness was, causing his body to notice…

Not that he'd do anything about it.

Even though he found her sweet, clean scent tempting. Very tempting.

He worried whether he'd keep that promise to himself as Melody shifted in her sleep, turning so she lay with her back against him.

Oh, yeah, he was warmer that way. Much warmer.

And sleep? With Melody so near him?

With her butt touching his most sensitive area, which reacted by doing anything but sleep thanks to that arousing contact?

With, in turn, his right arm under her head, his left arm over her shoulder…and his hand so very close to her full breasts?

Okay, he told himself after feeling he'd been awake for hours, but it had probably only been for half an hour. *Enough of this. Time to sleep.*

And somehow he managed to nod off.

Chapter 10

Was she the first to awaken? Melody believed so, just as she had yesterday morning.

Only then, they'd been in this same tent together, sure, but across from one another.

Now she was snuggled up against Casey on top of one of the sleeping bags, with the other one covering them. It felt good and warm and friendly, but nothing else, right?

And maybe her recollections of snuggling tighter against him, feeling his seeming arousal pressed tautly against her throughout most of the night, especially when she was just falling asleep, had been her imagination.

A dream.

A much too exciting dream…

Casey moved behind her…and she once again noticed what felt like an erection pushing into her back. She sucked in her breath, wondering if she should slide forward. Get up. At least move away…although she realized she liked that sensual pressure.

"Hey, Melody, are you awake?" Casey's deep, raspy voice startled her.

"Yes," she said, finally sliding forward because it seemed appropriate now. "I was wondering if you were."

"Yep. And I think it's still early enough for us to slip outside and see how the sunrise looks this morning."

He stood up first and held out his hand to help her stand. She could have gotten up just fine but appreciated his gentlemanliness, so she grasped his warm hand and was soon standing, though bent over in the tent, facing him.

They'd just spent the night together. Close. So close. But nothing untoward had happened—at least not on purpose.

Damn, but she appreciated the guy and his attitude.

Even as she found herself much too attracted to him and, as much as she disliked the idea under these circumstances, sexually frustrated.

Not that she'd let him know it. "First one out of this tent gets to choose what they'll eat for breakfast first."

"You're on." She was amused as, still in their heavy shirts, they both put on their shoes, then pretended to scramble for the flap. She got to push it open and recognized that Casey had held back so she'd be the winner. She considered doing something to let him out first, but then decided, what the heck? She got to see the sunrise first yesterday, so why not today?

Which she did. It wasn't quite as vivid as the prior morning's bright orange, but it seemed to be peach, striped with the white clouds. "Lovely," she breathed as she stood there, turning slightly to take it all in.

"Yes, lovely," Casey said beside her, but his throaty tone made her glance at him.

He was staring at her, but only until their eyes met. He looked away then and began studying the sky.

Was she just imagining that? Did he feel attracted to her the way she felt attracted to him?

Well, they had spent the night together. Very closely together. And he was a man. Definitely. Which meant his sexual instincts might even be more active than hers. Although hers...

Okay. Enough, she told herself. Without saying anything else to Casey she headed toward where Cal and Witchy were tethered, both of them now watching the humans. She unhitched Cal from the bush, while Casey did the same with Witchy, and they walked the horses to the nearby stream for a drink.

Yes, oddly, they seemed to be in somewhat of a routine out here on the ranch's extensive grounds. But they hadn't accomplished any of their goals yet.

They hadn't caught up with the stolen cattle even after two days.

That had to change. Somehow.

Did the rustlers know they were being followed?

Were they doing something to ultimately prevent it besides continuing forward?

Casey knew more about such things than she did, but she realized they needed to be careful. And do more to catch the criminals fast.

And Melody knew that she, as the experienced ranch hand in charge of this part of their expedition, had to decide what to do next to accomplish it.

Sure, that would eventually mean no more nights with Casey. But they needed to achieve their goal. And no longer being together?

Things would be better that way.

Although she truly would miss it.

They were out on the trail once more. As always—well, at least since this assignment had begun—Casey had first checked out the hoofprints they were following, which were a little more visible today in the drier grass of this area of the ranch's land.

Yes, Melody and he seemed to be heading in the right direction. Only this time, they weren't just following those hoofprints.

"Let me check the GPS," Melody had said a while back, before they'd had that day's breakfast.

She'd shown the map on her phone to him after they stopped. Yes, the cattle seemed to be on the move again. Still.

So they had a long way to go to catch up, even though Melody had suggested that they get the horses to go at a faster pace today, allowing for only brief rest stops. Her call, of course, since she knew the horses and the terrain best. But would that actually wind up in their going farther over the course of the day?

Casey wasn't sure. But somehow, they needed to get closer. Catch up.

Save those cattle a lot faster than things appeared to be going.

It felt like more than just his job now. It had also become his own personal goal.

"Our current routine hasn't gotten us far enough," Melody had told him, and that seemed true to him, too.

And now? Well, they'd also decided to take a slight detour—to check out the single separate dot showing on the GPS map, since they'd be passing it that day.

Had one of the cows lost her tag? It could still be sending a GPS signal even if it had been dropped onto the ground.

But they'd decided it was better to check it out, in case there was something at that site they needed to know—like an indication the thieves had discovered the sensors and were somehow allowing the others to send signals about false locations. Or maybe this was a test, where the rustlers had purposely left this one, along with someone observing it, to see if they were being followed.

They would have to be careful.

And in addition to everything else, it was Casey's job to ensure that Melody wouldn't come to any harm. Which felt as important to him—more so—than saving the cattle.

It wouldn't be surprising, after all, for the rustlers to know about the GPS. Many farms and ranches used it these days, according to Melody. "But if these rustlers know about it," Melody had said, "and if they have any smartness at all, they'd have done something to prevent the signal from showing us how they're progressing and the direction they're going."

Casey agreed but added, "If they can figure out how," and Melody had nodded.

"So if you weren't out here trying to catch cattle rustlers," Melody said a short while after they started off, possibly to break the silence, "what would you be doing?" She kept Cal walking right beside Witchy, and she looked witchingly good, tall in the saddle with her jeans and hoodie hugging her body…as he'd hugged her last night. And would like to continue doing even now.

Instead… "Not sure," he replied. "Guess it would depend on what kinds of crimes were going on in town, or at least what was suspected—or reported, rightly or wrongly. I'd most likely be sent to a location where a citizen reported a theft or even an assault, with or without a weapon. That seems to be my most usual assignment. Crime in Cactus Creek is fairly minimal, mostly thefts. Very few robberies or worse."

"And I assume you'd help the person who called as well as you could, depending on the crime and its status then, right?"

"Exactly."

"Which is your favorite kind of crime to investigate?" Melody asked. Judging by her expression as he looked at her again, she was actually interested in his answer, and he had to think quickly to come up with something that would amuse them both.

Maybe even something that was true.

"Battery," he said after a few seconds of pondering,

well aware of Witchy's clomping steps on the ground beneath them. "That's when someone—"

"Not only threatens to hit someone but actually does it, right?"

"Yes," he said, somewhat impressed. Many citizens didn't know the difference between battery and assault, which consisted of pretty much only the threat but no actual touching.

"But why do you like battery?" She sounded upset by the idea.

"I didn't mean that I *like* it," he clarified, "and even at that there are some kinds I prefer investigating over others. Not anything life-threatening, but I find it a tiny bit enjoyable to have to follow up on a call where someone complains of being hit by someone else, but it's sometimes because a kid used some kind of flexible toy these days—often a tube like they sometimes bring into in swimming pools, or a plastic bat."

When he looked over at Melody next, unsurprisingly still riding tall—and sexily, somehow—on Cal's back, she was staring at him skeptically. "Really?" she asked.

"No, not really." He grinned and used his heels to encourage Witchy to pick up her pace a little more.

They continued to converse as they rode, which Casey found himself enjoying, probably too much. He considered what he'd do when this assignment was complete and they didn't need to see each other professionally any more. Would he find a way to keep Melody in his life? No matter how much he was attracted to her out here, he hadn't changed his opinion about having any kind of romantic relationship, no matter who the woman was and how much he enjoyed her company.

And he did enjoy Melody's company. A lot. And getting to a point where he'd no longer see her?

Well, he didn't really want to think about that.

Just in case, he kept reminding himself of Georgia. Of her dumping him, and not just doing it any random time. No, she'd waited until the last moment, when they were just about to get married. When it would hurt him the worst.

No, he didn't need to risk anything like that ever again.

And besides, Melody was a new divorcée.

So she would be a good choice to continue developing a friendship with. Less risk with someone who'd also been there, done that, and come away with a similar attitude to his.

He realized his musing had caused a silence between them—one he needed to end. "Sorry," he said. "Just thinking of some of the battery cases I've looked into—and fortunately most of the perpetrators were arrested and found guilty at trial."

"The kids, too?" Melody asked, in a tone that told him she was joking.

"Oh, absolutely," he lied, then laughed. "No, I haven't tried prosecuting any kids."

And so their conversation went as they continued forward, sometimes discussing Melody's life as a ranch hand and her favorite part of it.

"Cleaning up a pasture after some members of the herd have been moved," she told him, her expression sincere…until he started laughing. Then she started laughing, too. "Or not," she said. "Instead, that could be my least favorite part."

"Got it," Casey acknowledged. As he did often, he scanned the mostly green pasture they were traversing at a quicker pace than they had over the last couple of days. This part seemed more irregular than some of the locations, with its deeply rolling hillsides and even more areas with bushes. Plus the grass was pretty long except where it had been worn down right around them by the cattle who'd been driven through here. He doubted that many cattle were brought out here to graze.

It shouldn't be too long, he figured, until they reached the area where that one lone red dot appeared on the GPS app.

That was Melody's take, too, he assumed when she slowed Cal down a bit and pulled her cell phone from her pocket. Holding the reins more loosely, she looked at the screen and swiped it.

"We're almost there," she said. "Let's head a little to our right. Whatever's causing the dot to appear in my GPS tracker is just over that hill." She pointed ahead, but unsurprisingly toward their right.

"No further indication of what it is?" he asked, even knowing that greater detail, even close by, was highly unlikely on a GPS map.

"Nope, though it's likely to be a cow—or just the GPS tag that's somehow been taken off. We'll find out soon."

And they did. The result clearly upset Melody. A lot. For as soon as their horses walked over the small ridge nearest the dot's location and they could see the grass-covered part of the hillside beyond, the cow that was wearing the tag was visible.

Lying there, on the ground.

Clearly dead.

"No!" Melody quickly urged Cal to get closer, then slid off the saddle from her horse's back. There were bushes close by, so she quickly tied Cal to the nearest one and kneeled near where the black Angus cow was lying on the ground, unmoving, a mat of darkness against the otherwise green-and-brown surface below her.

And yes, it was a her, undoubtedly one of the female cattle they were chasing.

What had happened to her?

And what were they going to do about her?

Melody would definitely have to notify Clarence, and soon—but not until she had more answers for him.

She moved around on her jeans-clad knees on the roughness of the dirt and the little bit of grass above it until she reached the cow's head. Wincing, she nevertheless reached forward until she had the poor creature's ear in her hand. It felt cold, despite the warm air surrounding her. No warmth of life. And, fortunately, no smell of death—at least not yet.

With a sigh, Melody gently massaged that ear, anyway, not because the cow could feel anything but because Melody needed the information from the tag concealed at the back of her ear. She knew it still had to be there, for why else would the GPS have picked up this location?

She noticed then that she wasn't alone kneeling on the ground beside the dead member of the herd she'd been seeking. Casey was beside her, one arm around her back as she continued to lean forward and caress the cow's closest ear, her left one. The other ear was beneath her head, against the ground. Fortunately, the OverHerd cattle's tags were always attached to the left ear. Otherwise, they'd have had to find a way to lift that heavy head and maybe even the front part of the body.

And, oddly, the brand at the back of the poor cow's side, near her tail, looked off. This had to be one of the OverHerd stock, yet instead of displaying OHR, some of the hair around it had been singed differently, and somehow so had the skin beneath. It now said SG.

What ranch was that?

"Can you tell yet what happened?" Casey asked.

"No. I'll do what I can here to check, but I'm no expert in anything medical." But she did finally feel the small tag by the cow's ear and, though she hated to move away from the comforting feel of Casey beside her, she edged closer and looked down.

It was well camouflaged, so it was entirely possible that the rustlers weren't aware of it. But Melody could read it. The poor cow was Addie. Melody had worked with her before. Now, Melody stopped herself from giving her a hug while she attempted to study the tag.

She also tried to remove it before Casey said, "Don't do that. It's potential evidence in this crime. In fact, don't touch it."

"Of course," she agreed. She took a picture of it with her phone, although the tag's text was hard to read that way. She would grab some paper and a pen from her saddlebag soon and jot down the number on the tag that confirmed the cow's identity.

She could notify Clarence of both, let him know that they'd found one of the stolen cattle—and what condition she was in.

But Melody really wanted to know why. And so, before rising again, she started crawling around on her knees, examining all she could of poor Addie—

And then, as she moved a bit more, looking at the cow's head from a different angle, she saw it: the hole in the middle of her forehead, above the closed eyes. It was a little difficult to see in the cow's black fur. Only the tiniest bit of blood had seeped from it.

She pointed it out to Casey, who also remained on the ground but not right at her side. Instead, he was nearer the cow's still legs and hooves.

"There," Melody said, hearing the hoarseness in her own tone. Not surprising, considering her sorrow. And anger. "That may be what caused her death. Is it…do you think it's a bullet hole?"

She held her breath, hardly wanting to look toward that hole and not choosing to see the expression on the face of the deputy who was with her. He had a lot more experience, she presumed, with recognizing bullet holes.

"Yeah," he said. "I just noticed that myself and… well, I wasn't sure I should point it out to you."

"Of course you should." Melody felt affronted. She

needed to know all she could about what had happened, all the details possible.

Even the most horrible ones.

"Then, yes. Best I could tell, that's a bullet hole. And would you like my take on why someone shot that cow?"

"Yes." Melody had an urge to shout at Casey. Tell him off for treating her like some fragile little woman and not revealing all he knew or suspected to her.

She needed to know it all.

Casey turned to point somewhat behind him...and Melody saw at once what he was pointing at.

One of the cow's limbs seemed extended in the wrong direction. Had she broken her leg?

That would have given the rustlers reason to leave her here, since she couldn't have kept up with them.

Was slaying her somehow an act of kindness to prevent her suffering? Melody shuddered. Nothing about this was kind. It was horrible that the cattle had been stolen and herded along out here—

And that this one had somehow been injured and therefore killed.

"I—I see," she said softly to Casey. "I think you're right. I need to let Clarence know what we found, right away. I doubt he'll send a team here immediately but he might want to. First, though, I want to look around here a little more. I doubt there are any more dead cattle, with just the one GPS dot showing up, but I'd like to see if I can tell how this one got hurt in the first place and if there's anything else I need to tell Clarence."

"Fine. I'll stay with you."

Which she appreciated. She pulled herself up to a standing position, and Casey did the same. Then she looked down again at Addie.

Melody felt terribly sad for her. She'd suffered an injury and then been killed because of it.

"You poor thing," she whispered, then looked around.

Casey had started walking away—he was heading toward a row of uneven bushes at the edges. She was unsure why he pursued that track. Had the cow somehow slipped there? But how had Addie wound up back here, at the top?

Maybe they'd never find out exactly what had happened. Melody pulled her phone from her pocket again and took some pictures of the poor, dead cow.

Then she followed Casey toward the slope.

He waited for her there, holding out his hand. "This does look a bit treacherous, though that cow must somehow have been injured up there since the rustlers probably couldn't have gotten her back to the top otherwise. But we can go down to check it out." It was, in fact, a fairly steep slope, one that a cow probably could not walk down safely without assistance, Melody believed.

"Fine," she said, then took another couple of pictures from this angle, before they started down.

And then—

Casey must have seen what Melody did at the same time. "Damn!" he exclaimed, still holding her hand as they began to hurry as much as they could on this dangerous incline.

"No!" Melody shouted, pulling ahead of Casey as

much as she could without falling. She shoved her phone back into her pocket—for now.

In moments, she bent down over the horrible thing in front of her.

"Pierce?" Melody called out as she kneeled beside the body of the kind, smart ranch hand who'd pretty much been her mentor. Her friend. She felt as if she had been punched in the gut. She had felt sorry about the dead cow—but Pierce? Surely he would be okay, right?

She grabbed his wrist to try to find a pulse, but with his pallor, his lack of breathing or any other movement, and what she saw, she knew the answer.

There was a similar hole in the middle of his forehead, but much more noticeable than the one on the cow. Blood had flowed from it…and was visible on his ashen face.

Pierce Tostig was dead.

Chapter 11

Casey immediately dove into deputy mode. He kneeled down to check for any indication the victim was still alive and found nothing. Even so, just in case, he quickly started CPR, but when chest compressions still had no effect, he noted in his mind the location and the hour—one in the afternoon—though he wouldn't be the one to determine the time of death.

Now he realized Melody had begun sobbing beside him. How well had she known the guy? No matter. They'd clearly at least been coworkers and probably friends.

Would she cry so much if he was injured...or worse? Casey didn't want to find out, yet on one level he hoped she cared enough about him to do so.

Ridiculous.

He kept performing CPR a short while longer, then stopped and decided it was time to make a call.

He stood up and Melody stood beside him, not looking down toward the body. Her eyes were red, her cheeks damp, but she was no longer crying.

"What—what should we do now?" she asked him.

"I need to phone this in. My department will undoubtedly send a team out here as fast as possible to deal with the situation."

She nodded. "I understand…though getting out here will be a challenge." She pulled her own phone out of her pocket but just held it against her chest for a moment. Then, clearly tense and upset, she looked down and took a picture before turning away again and putting back her phone. "I'll wait to hear what's happening before I call Clarence and let him know."

"Good idea."

Still watching her, he pulled his own phone from his pocket. He hoped it still had reception this far out, though since Melody's did, at least enough for her GPS to work, surely his would, too—right?

Fortunately, the answer was yes. He immediately called Sheriff Krester directly. Also fortunately, he answered right away.

Casey put the call on speaker, since he thought Melody might be able to contribute to it as far as how to find them.

"Hi, Casey," his boss said. "I didn't expect to hear from you till tonight, since—"

"We've just come across a dead body, sir," Casey interrupted.

"What? Who. And where?"

Casey explained the circumstances as quickly and succinctly as he could, including that he was still with Melody, and they continued to search for the missing herd of cattle.

"So you think the cow's death and that ranch hand's are related?" the sheriff asked.

"They must be, since they died so close together and so similarly, but I have no idea why, at least regarding Pierce."

"Well, we obviously need to bring Pierce's body back here to have it checked out first by medical personnel, then by the coroner. How do you propose we do that?"

Good question, Casey thought. "We're out here on horseback, as you know. And we'd already determined that anything in the air like a plane or helicopter would give away our location and let the thieves know we're chasing them. But—"

"Under these circumstances," Melody interrupted, "I'd like to suggest that you use a helicopter. If you send it from around the ranch and in the same direction we've been going, and keep it relatively low, the rustlers aren't likely to see it. I gather they're still some distance ahead of us and the terrain between them and us rolls a lot. And maybe if you use a helicopter that isn't marked as part of the sheriff's department, they won't worry as much if they see it, anyway—assuming they could see any markings on it."

"Good idea," Casey said, admiring his partner in this search, though that was nothing new. He'd had a similar thought but didn't know the terrain as well as she did. "Of course, if they see any indication of a chopper they'll probably figure that the body they left here has been found."

"But they won't know how or by who, or that the people who found it are following them," Melody said. "Although...well, we really need to be careful. If they get too suspicious, they may kill the remaining cattle and disappear before we catch them."

That wasn't a new concern, but voicing it again to Jeremy couldn't hurt. Another reason for Casey to admire Melody.

And he felt certain that she wanted no further harm to come to the missing herd—or any other person.

"Okay," Jeremy said. "We'll send a chopper right away. It wouldn't do to leave a body out there, plus you need to stay with it till it's been picked up rather than continuing on your trail. I'll get something going and call you back."

"Yes, sir," Casey said, and then, after a few more brief comments and questions, they hung up.

"Guess we'll see a helicopter soon," Melody said. He noticed that her beautiful and sad brown eyes had seemed glued to him during the whole conversation. Surely it was because she didn't want to look down at her fallen comrade rather than for any other reason.

"Guess so." Because it was the right thing to do— and because it might help Melody cope a little better with their discovery of her friend's body—Casey kneeled, pulled off Pierce's black sweatshirt and put it over his face.

She wasn't watching, he noticed. Though she'd taken

a picture of Pierce lying there, she now seemed disinclined to look down at all. In fact, she had taken her phone from her pocket again. She pressed a button and Casey figured she must feel it was time to notify her boss about what had happened out here.

Bad stuff. He'd been assigned to find missing cattle, not deal with a murder. Oh, but he definitely would help to solve it. But this shouldn't happen anywhere, let alone around Cactus Creek.

Melody felt her eyes tear up again as she pressed the button on her phone to call Clarence.

A small portion of her distress was because of having to make this call. Her boss was more than the owner of the important, lucrative ranch that she worked for. He was also a big man in town, its selectman, and he expected everyone to recognize his importance and do what was necessary to comply with promises made to him—and she was about to deliver bad news.

At the moment, though, she'd been handed a particularly important job. But all she'd done so far was help locate a cow who'd been injured and killed. And worse, much worse, she had also helped to find the body of another ranch hand, one more important than she was, who'd probably come out here on his own, intending to be a lot more successful than she'd been in bringing down the rustlers. Well, he'd apparently found them first.

Enough. If Clarence wanted to fire her for being ineffective—and finding Pierce—so be it. She glanced toward Casey, who was watching her, probably reading, in the expression on her face, her sorrow at her failure—and, worse, in finding poor Pierce's body. Pierce, who'd always been so kind to her, who'd helped her learn what she needed to about this ranch and its livestock.

Surely he'd been out here attempting, like her, to find the missing cattle—and hadn't been involved in their disappearance. She refused to believe that.

She made herself take one deep breath, then another. Casey had allowed her to participate in his conversation with his boss, and she believed she'd actually been of some use.

Following his example, she made herself give him a small smile as they continued to stand there, their backs toward the area where poor Pierce was lying, and pushed the buttons on her phone to call Clarence and put the conversation on the speaker.

She half hoped this would be one of those times when Clarence didn't answer first thing...but he did.

"Okay, Melody," he began, "I'm surprised to hear from you in the middle of the day. Does this mean you've actually made some progress?"

She winced at the criticism in his voice and his tone, allowing herself to glance slightly sideways to see Casey's reaction.

"Hello, Selectman Edison," Casey intoned in a chilly voice. "This is Deputy Sheriff Casey Colton. I'm here with Melody, and we have a couple of matters you should be informed about."

A slight pause, then Clarence said, "What matters?"

Melody suspected that their finding the body of one of his precious cows would be of greater importance to him than the fact they'd also discovered Pierce's body, even though he'd been one of Clarence's employees. Nevertheless, she said, "Sir, we have unfortunately discovered the body of one of your senior ranch hands, Pierce Tostig. We're not sure why he was here—probably trying to help by looking for the missing herd, too—but we found him near the dead body of one of the cows."

"What! Tell me more about this—the cow and Pierce."

Melody wasn't surprised at the order in which he asked about them. She shot a glance toward Casey, whose expression appeared full of irony as he shook his head slightly. He'd caught that Clarence had put the animal before the man.

Melody opened her mouth to begin relating what they'd been through but Casey beat her to it. He described how they had first come upon the corpse of the poor cow, how its leg had been broken and that it apparently had been shot as a result. They had started looking around the area for any ideas about who'd done it and when—and that was when they had discovered Pierce's corpse.

"Was he the one who shot the cow?" Clarence demanded, his tone suggesting he'd have gladly shot his employee, too, if he'd discovered the dead cow first.

"I don't know," Melody said. "It's possible that he found the poor, injured cow and decided to prevent her from suffering anymore."

"And someone decided to prevent him from suffering any more, too," Clarence said almost pleasantly, as if he was nodding his head back in the town at the appropriateness of the act.

Again Melody met Casey's gaze, and she cringed at the anger she saw there. "Anyway," she said hastily, "the sheriff's department is going to come here to pick up poor Pierce's body. We'll need to leave the cow here for now because there's no good way to take her back to the ranch, especially since we're still hoping the rustlers won't realize we're out here and chasing them."

"Then hurry up and catch them already," Clarence shouted, making Melody move the phone farther from her ear. "I don't want you to wind up finding any more of my valuable stock out there dead, you hear me?"

"Yes, sir." Melody did her best to keep the annoyance she felt out of her tone. But she couldn't joke, either. "And I'll keep you informed as we continue, though not tonight. 'Bye."

And then she hung up—and felt those damn tears return to her eyes again.

She was grieving—for Pierce, of course, and the cow...as well as the peacefulness of her own life.

She again caught Casey's gaze, even as he took several steps toward her. Neither of them was looking down.

In a moment, she was in his arms as he gave her a hug. She hugged him back. She knew they were sharing sympathy and empathy and sorrow. She needed that.

And wondered how she was going to survive this assignment with her sanity in place.

Casey didn't know the helicopter pilot or the EMTs—a man and a woman—who appeared at the site not much more than half an hour later, landing on the nearby pasture. He did appreciate the quick arrival and how they immediately got to work checking out Pierce and confirming that he was deceased—no question in Casey's mind about that, either, as unfortunate as it was. This was definitely a homicide, and a full investigation would need to be commenced. Casey could only hope it would be solved fast and the perpetrator prosecuted quickly. A couple members of the sheriff's department were along, too, and Casey knew them. He was surprised that one of them was Deputy Bob Andrews, the young guy who mostly hung out at the department answering the phone and greeting people who came in, then sending the more experienced deputies out on calls. Maybe this was to be a learning experience for him, since he was unlikely to accomplish much.

But Casey wasn't surprised that he was accompanied by Captain Walter Forman, who had a lot more seniority than Casey, and was even nearing retirement. Most important, he was one of the most experienced investigators in the department.

Well, Walter might have more experience, but Casey was already involved in this situation. He intended to remain a primary investigator out here, even while continuing to hunt for the missing cattle.

He hoped to be the one to find the answers.

As the EMTs got busy checking Pierce, Walter had Bob take a lot of pictures. He then began asking both Casey and Melody questions about how they'd gotten here, what they'd seen, how they'd found Pierce's body and more. Casey knew how to respond efficiently and did so, and was glad to hear Melody do so as well. Bob asked a few questions, too, furthering Casey's assumption that he was along partly to help but probably also to learn more of what an investigation was like.

On Walter's request, they took Bob and him up the rise to look at the dead cow while they left the EMTs and helicopter pilot near the site where they'd discovered Pierce's body. Melody led the group, and Casey enjoyed watching her athletic body, in her hoodie and jeans, navigate along the rise. Casey assumed she wanted to spend as much time with what was left of the cow that she could—or at least point out what she could about the poor animal's condition.

Their horses, fortunately, were still tethered close by, which prompted Casey to ask Walter some questions of his own. "Do you have any knowledge about how Mr. Tostig got out here? Are you aware whether he also rode a horse here from the ranch? Ours are here, but we didn't see any others."

"No, we're not aware yet how he got here," Walter said. "Or even why, although we gather he may have gone after the missing cattle on his own, without approval from anyone at the ranch. We already have a team at the ranch asking questions, and I'll make sure they check to see if Mr. Tostig was out here on horseback, which seems logical. Maybe while you're out on the range, you can keep an eye out for his missing horse as well as the cattle. And once Bob and I complete what investigation we can out here we'll head back to the ranch, too, after Mr. Tostig's body has been taken to the morgue."

They'd reached the cow's corpse, and flies buzzed

around it now. Melody swiped at them with her hand, then said, "I know Clarence will want to see this cow himself or at least send someone out here from the ranch to deal with her body. Is there some way we can cover her up for now, keep her as clean as possible?"

"We've got some blankets in the helicopter and could use those," Bob said.

"Thank you." Melody looked down again at the cow and shook her head slightly. Casey assumed she was crying again, or at least fighting not to, so he approached and put his arm around her. He doubted he'd be much comfort, but at least he could try.

She looked at him. Sure enough, her eyes were shimmering, but she took a deep breath and smiled at him. "This is hard. I don't know how you can hang out at crime scenes helping people or doing what else you do and keep your sanity."

"Who says I'm sane?" he quipped, and her smile grew even larger.

After answering a few more of Walter's—and Bob's—questions, they returned to the area below. Pierce's body had been removed, and Casey assumed he was inside the helicopter. Walter told Bob to go inside and get the blankets to cover the cow.

Casey figured Melody and he had helped around here all they could, answering questions and showing the other members of his department around.

They were through here, as far as he was concerned, although he didn't know how long the others intended to stay.

No matter. Melody and he had their own assignment to resume.

He approached Walter, who was taking more pictures with his phone of the barren area where Pierce's body had been. "Melody and I are going to get on our way now," Casey told him. "There's even more reason now to locate the missing cattle and the people who stole them."

"Very true," Walter said. "Only…well, we'll do the same thing with the chopper when we leave as when we arrived here. I'll make sure our pilot heads the same direction we came from and keeps it low and hopefully not too noticeable. But who knows where the killers are? You'll need to be careful. And once I've done my report, it's entirely possible that Sheriff Krester will want to send a whole unit out in the direction you're heading, maybe in another chopper, even if it's seen by the thieves. We definitely need to apprehend them now, since the only evidence we have points to them as the probable murderers."

"I understand," Melody said. She'd been speaking with Bob, who now held some blankets off to the side of where Casey stood with Walter, but she must have been listening. "But, please, give us another day or two and keep in touch with us. I'm just afraid that when the rustlers realize Pierce has been found and people are definitely after them, they'll kill the remaining cattle, too."

"Let's hope not," Walter said, sending Melody a sympathetic look. "But I'm sure you realize that catching a perpetrator after a murder investigation will have to take precedence."

"I understand," she repeated, "and I appreciate your covering that cow up with those." She looked first at Bob, who nodded as he moved the blankets around. She then turned to look Casey straight in the eye. "Please, please, let's get going now."

Being here, finding first the cow, then poor Pierce, had been hard. Very hard. But also motivating.

Melody had obviously wanted to find the rustlers before. Now, Casey believed she felt it was even more important.

Well, so did he. Oh, yeah. It was time to get going.

Chapter 12

Bouncing a bit as her horse navigated the rougher grass-and-dirt terrain, Melody had an urge to press her heels harder against Cal's sides and get him to gallop. And if Cal sped forward, Witchy would, too.

But for now, she continued at their current pace, which was the fastest they had traveled so far on this fiasco of a search.

Why? Why had nice, helpful Pierce been killed? And why had he even been out there?

What did his death have to do with the poor cow being killed?

And where was Pierce's horse...assuming he'd had one? How else would he have gotten there, in the middle of nowhere? Perhaps the rustlers had another helicopter that Casey and she hadn't seen?

All the more reason to catch up with those horrible thieves…and most likely murderers, since who else would have killed Pierce?

At least she believed they were still going the right way. She'd checked the GPS on her phone before they got back on their horses and headed in the same direction they'd been going before the horrible interruption they'd just experienced. Sure enough, the cluster of small red dots was ahead of them—still way ahead of them and continuing to move, but maybe not as fast as before if Melody was interpreting correctly. And they didn't seem to have changed course. No further small dots on their own, fortunately.

But who knew what would happen next? More animal killings?

More murders?

That had now been several hours ago. After their delay, they only had another hour or so before they'd have to stop because of darkness.

"You doing okay?" Casey asked from beside her.

"Yes," she said, then felt herself grimace. "And no. I'm getting really tired of this outing." Well, not entirely. She was enjoying his company. But still— "I want answers. Results. Saving those poor cattle out there and letting you arrest the damn people who—who killed…"

She knew she was about to cry again, and so she forced her gaze to go forward without finishing her sentence.

"I'm so sorry, Melody," Casey said, his tone bleak enough that she had to look at him. "I should have insisted from the first that only people from my department should be out here doing this. We'd have found a way to deal with crossing the land even without knowing much about the terrain. The GPS signal should have been enough."

"No!" Melody exclaimed, then repeated more softly, "No. That's not what I'm trying to say. You didn't know Pierce was coming. None of us did. And having one of the hands from OverHerd officially along with you was the best way to do this. I'm glad I was the one chosen. It's just that…well, I understood the possibility of finding some of the cattle injured or even killed under these circumstances. But another one of the ranch hands? I hadn't considered that. And what if Pierce had been the one to accompany you instead? He certainly knew this terrain as well as I do, probably better. I know he had lots more responsibilities at the ranch he needed to tend to, so in some ways it made sense for me to go along, but maybe he'd still be alive if—"

"I understand why you're doing this," Casey interrupted. "You're trying to figure out how to deal with what happened, but coming up with a way to blame yourself won't work. It won't bring Pierce back, or even Addie the cow. Best thing we can do is to continue along here, get to the herd and deal with the bad guys, and the cattle, in the best way possible once we recognize what that is."

"You're right." Melody looked across the short distance between their mounts, appreciating Casey's attempt to make her feel better. It actually helped, at least a little.

And she was determined to ensure, in whatever way

she could, that they were successful in catching the rustlers. And bringing them to justice for killing Pierce. That would also make them pay for what they did to Addie.

"Come on," she said. "Let's step up the pace a bit more, okay? I'm beginning to see some color on the clouds at the horizon and the sky's not as bright as it was before. Sunset's getting close."

"You're right, as I gather you usually are. So—" He suddenly pressed his heels against Witchy's side, and his horse sped up.

"Let's go, Cal," she said and did the same thing.

But she would only allow it for about twenty minutes. She didn't want the horses to get too tired or injure themselves.

They'd have an even bigger day tomorrow, she figured. Their pace would be like this, on and off, for much more of the day.

Would they finally catch up with the rustlers?

Oh, yes, she told herself, realizing she might not be realistic. But she'd do all she could to ensure that came true. It was certainly about time.

When she finally started slowing down Cal and calling to Casey to do the same with Witchy, they'd fortunately reached another area where the vast, rolling pasture was broken up with patches of underbrush as well as thick, tall bushes. Plus there was a pond nearby with a small creek flowing through it, which would be great for the horses and for their own preparations and ablutions that night.

The main problem would be the same anywhere

around here. The air was already growing chilly and would only get colder.

But things could be worse. The clouds in the sky were few and did not appear dark. That was one thing that had worked in their favor these days and nights— no rain.

"How's this?" she asked Casey, waving her arm to encompass the area she was contemplating.

"Looks good to me," he said. "It'll be only a short while 'til the sun's completely down. Let's get ready… and plan to leave here as early in the morning as possible."

"Great," Melody said and directed Cal, who was now just walking, toward an open spot that was clear in the middle of some areas decorated with underbrush. It was large enough that they could attach the horses right there and also put up their tent for some semblance of cover.

Hard to think it was nearly time for bed, getting their tent—their single tent—set up so they would rest together again that night, but yes, they needed to get to sleep fast so they could get as early a start as possible in the morning.

They began what Melody now considered their routine. Would this be the last night for it? She hoped so, despite how she had come to enjoy it—performing silly, small chores alongside her comrade in this chase.

And she forced herself not to consider how much she would miss it—and him—when they were finally successful.

In a short while, they'd dismounted from their horses,

unsaddled them, removed the bits from their mouths, and walked them to the pond, tying them there. Then Casey and she set up their small tent nearby.

By the time they'd taken care of themselves, filtered some water for drinking by the horses and them and made paltry attempts at bathing—clothes on, of course, although with lifting and unbuttoning and replacing a lot of the time—the sky was nearly dark. And despite herself, Melody had tried peeking at Casey but hadn't seen anything exciting.

Melody checked again on the horses and figured that where they were currently tethered should work for the night and would allow them to drink from the containers of filtered water at their leisure. She again gave them some of the grain she had brought, although they shouldn't be hungry considering the amount of time they'd been tied up at the grassy area where… Melody moved her mind away from that as much as she could and let herself dwell on the other times Casey and she had slowed down or stopped to allow the horses to rest—and eat—a bit.

She looked around and, not seeing Casey, figured he was inside the tent. Glancing at it, she saw the fabric on the top moving a little, confirming her presumption.

Another night was coming up when she'd be alone with Casey. Would they snuggle together to stay warm as they had last night? She hoped so.

She could use a little human contact for other reasons, too, after this very difficult day.

Particularly with this man, who was becoming an important part of her life.

For now, she assured herself. Just for now.

In a moment she, too, had bent over and made her way inside the tent. She kneeled on the dirt floor, although one of the sleeping bags was already spread out on the ground not far away.

Casey had also turned on the lanterns.

"Ready to eat?" she asked, walking forward on her knees to where the saddlebags rested on the ground to her left.

"Always," Casey said. "I'll be glad when I can take you to a nice restaurant for a salad and a real meal."

"Or I'll take you," Melody said. And how enjoyable would that be? Going on a date with this man might not be appropriate, but she felt sure it would be fun. "After all, your assignment now may be to chase bad guys, but it's also to help out our town selectman. We can let him treat."

She watched a shadowed grin appear on Casey's handsome, somewhat bearded face and had to smile back.

"Sounds good to me," he said. "I guess we can order some pretty tasty steaks at his expense, right?"

"Right."

She wasn't sure what Clarence would think of something like that, but figured that if—when—Casey and she returned to Cactus Creek after successfully tracking down and apprehending the bad guys and, even more importantly, bringing back the remaining valuable cattle, her boss wouldn't blink an eye at granting them some kind of reward. A good dinner should surely be on the agenda.

But for the time being, they again pulled out the bottles of filtered water for that evening as well as the standard fare of dried fruit, carrots and celery, trail mix, energy bars and some beef jerky, which they hadn't snacked on much since they hadn't brought a lot of it.

They both sat on opposite ends of the sleeping bag that was stretched out beneath them. Melody reached for something to say. They'd probably exhausted talking about their pasts. Maybe their hopes for the future… besides capturing the rustlers and saving the cattle?

Actually, she was willing to talk about nearly anything, wanted to talk about nearly anything—except what had happened that day.

"So," Casey said, waving a half-eaten energy bar in the air. "Once we're finally through with all this, I'll visit you on your ranch again, but even more important, I'd like you to come see me at the sheriff's department. I'll want to show my fellow deputies who they could have been helping if they'd been the ones to volunteer for this little task."

Interesting. Casey assumed they would see one another again after they'd completed their task together. Melody had begun to hope for it but doubted it would happen. But if Casey wanted it, too?

"Did you volunteer for 'this little task'?" Melody asked, to keep the conversation going appropriately. She had gotten the impression that the sheriff had pressed him into service for this assignment, without any choice. But right now, she figured that Casey was searching for a noncontroversial, nonemotional topic for them to talk about, and she appreciated it.

"Well, no," he replied, "but I would have, if I'd known someone like you would be my contact out here. And, hey, we're about to spend our third night together."

Which made Melody laugh…just a little. She also, unsurprisingly, thought about what he'd said, what he'd reminded her about unnecessarily.

She was about to spend yet another night with Casey, one where they hopefully would snuggle again for warmth.

But she had a feeling it wouldn't be easy to stay remote from him again. Still. Not after everything that had occurred that day.

Having someone to hold her had never sounded better. But more? She recognized that having his hard body against her tonight might be enough to get her to try to forget all the bad things in exchange for something special.

Which she recognized was impossible. Touching him, making love with him, was absolutely prohibited. She couldn't let her sorrow toss her into something she definitely didn't want.

Or maybe, if she acknowledged it to herself, she did want…too much. But she definitely didn't want a relationship with another man. Not so soon after her divorce. So why even consider getting physical?

Except…well, maybe it would in some way help her deal with that sorrow.

"Look, Melody." Casey inched closer and took her hands into his. "I just want to…well, apologize in a way, even though there was nothing I could do to prevent what happened today. But I assume you and Pierce were pretty close. And—"

She glanced into Casey's wonderful, sympathetic blue eyes, and didn't—couldn't—look away. "In a way, yes—as mentor-protégée, I guess, though I already knew a lot about ranching before I came here. But Pierce was the main hand here to teach me about this particular ranch. We became good buddies."

"So I'm sure what happened to him was even harder for you than if he'd simply been a fellow ranch hand you worked with now and then."

Casey's gaze changed slightly—was it hardening? Questioning? Was he making the wrong assumption? Maybe he was allowing himself to believe that she and Pierce had some kind of romantic relationship, which would stop anything from potentially occurring between them.

But she wouldn't imply a relationship that didn't exist. Casey and she had to have only truth between them, she told herself.

Especially if the untruth somehow flipped their rapport into distance.

Her voice, when she responded, was soft and raspy, but she continued to look straight into Casey's eyes. "To me, Pierce was just another ranch hand—a special one, sure, and one whose help I appreciated. But I'd have felt this bad if the same thing happened to any of my coworkers. Our connection is always special, but it's all wrapped up in making sure the cattle are treated as well as possible."

"Which is why you were so upset about finding that dead cow," Casey acknowledged.

"Exactly. It's kind of a strange bond among all of the ranch hands and to some degree the animals we care for. I don't know what it's like for you as a sheriff's deputy, but maybe you can relate what I feel to losing another peace officer you knew, or maybe a victim you tried to help." She couldn't help hesitating. "That could be an exaggeration, I know. But—"

The expression on his face changed again, this time to what appeared to be even greater sympathy. "Exaggeration or not, I get it," he said, and suddenly he moved closer so there was no longer any gap between them.

They sat for an instant facing each other, close up. And then...well, Melody wasn't sure which of them reached out first, but suddenly they were kneeling again, in each other's arms, tightly, sensually, as their lips met in a kiss that was far more than any sympathetic gesture between friends who'd suffered difficult circumstances together.

Casey's mouth was hot and searching on hers, and Melody couldn't help responding in kind, wanting to experience all she could by this wonderful kiss.

But their position on the sleeping bag, as they pushed up against one another, felt awkward.

And Melody knew just what to do about it.

Gently but firmly, keeping her arms around Casey, she pulled him down so they were both lying on top of that sleeping bag, still kissing heatedly.

She enjoyed the feel of his growing beard against her skin. And in moments their tongues were playing an exploratory touching game that made Melody's insides begin to sizzle, then burn when one of Casey's hands moved down her back and grasped her butt.

"Oh," she gasped, even as her own hands began to move, partly by design and partly because, instinctively, she wanted—needed—to touch him as sensuously as he was touching her.

And that desire was triggered even more when, as they drew closer, she felt a hardness press into her stomach, a sexual stimulus sparked by her recognizing his erection but wanting to feel it more.

Maybe even see it.

But before she could pull away to reach between them, she felt Casey tugging gently at the back of her jeans. "Don't worry, I'll keep you warm," he said, barely moving his mouth away from hers.

She couldn't help smiling a little. "And I'll keep you warm," she said. "No—*hot*."

For she realized then, appropriate or not, what they were about to do.

In moments, they were both nude. The air was chilly around them, but at least there was no breeze inside the tent. And they remained so close to one another, first touching bared skin, then reaching for the other's most sensitive parts.

Hardly aware of where they were or anything else except that she was with Casey, and what she'd been wanting without allowing herself to acknowledge it seemed about to occur.

Casey caressed Melody's breasts first and her nipples hardened beneath his fingers. She gasped and used the stimulus to move her own hands to his most sexy places, first his now-nude butt, then around to his erection.

She inhaled with more than a gasp at the feel of its length, its hardness, beneath her fingers. As he made a noise that sounded like the most sensuous moan she had ever heard, she stroked him with a pumping motion that imitated what she wanted him to do…within her.

Instead, she almost shouted in frustration as he pulled away, rolling over so his back was to her and he faced his saddlebag. What? He was hungry for food again now rather than—

But he soon turned back, something in his hand.

A condom.

He'd anticipated this? Or was it just another way this accomplished deputy sheriff stayed prepared for anything?

Instead of shouting, she smiled again. "Let me," she said as she reached for it, then pulled away the wrapping. Unrolling the condom upon his amazingly hard length turned her on as much as anything she had ever experienced.

Until, moments later, he was on top of her, kissing, sucking her breasts…and then he reached below to caress her most sensitive parts. "Oh, Casey," she moaned, then gasped again as he moved again and carefully but insistently pressed himself inside her.

She could hardly think during the next…how long was it? Hours? Moments? She felt no sense of time, only touching and heat and desire as Casey's movements increased in speed and intensity…until his body stopped moving and he moaned.

Even as she felt herself come, too.

And as Melody soon lay there beside Casey, still enjoying his closeness, she wondered how their working together would be over the next day or two.

She felt certain nothing between them would ever be the same again.

"FAST FIVE" READER SURVEY

Your participation entitles you to:
✴ 4 Thank-You Gifts Worth Over $20!

Complete the survey in minutes.

Get **2 FREE** Books

Your Thank-You Gifts include **2 FREE BOOKS** and **2 MYSTERY GIFTS**. There's no obligation to purchase anything!

See inside for details.

Dear Reader,

Since you are a lover of our books, your opinions are important to us... and so is your time.

That's why we made sure your **"FAST FIVE" READER SURVEY** can be completed in just a few minutes. Your answers to the five questions will help us remain at the forefront of women's fiction.

And, as a thank-you for participating, we'd like to send you **4 FREE THANK-YOU GIFTS!**

Enjoy your gifts with our appreciation,

Pam Powers

To get your
4 FREE THANK-YOU GIFTS:

✹ Quickly complete the "Fast Five" Reader Survey
and return the insert.

"FAST FIVE" READER SURVEY

1	Do you sometimes read a book a second or third time?	○ Yes ○ No
2	Do you often choose reading over other forms of entertainment such as television?	○ Yes ○ No
3	When you were a child, did someone regularly read aloud to you?	○ Yes ○ No
4	Do you sometimes take a book with you when you travel outside the home?	○ Yes ○ No
5	In addition to books, do you regularly read newspapers and magazines?	○ Yes ○ No

YES! I have completed the above Reader Survey. Please send me my 4 FREE GIFTS (gifts worth over $20 retail). I understand that I am under no obligation to buy anything, as explained on the back of this card.

240/340 HDL GNPN

FIRST NAME	LAST NAME

ADDRESS

APT.#	CITY

STATE/PROV.	ZIP/POSTAL CODE

READER SERVICE—Here's how it works:

◄ If offer card is missing write to: Reader Service, P.O. Box 1341, Buffalo, NY 14240-8531 or visit www.ReaderService.com ◄

BUSINESS REPLY MAIL
FIRST-CLASS MAIL   PERMIT NO. 717   BUFFALO, NY

POSTAGE WILL BE PAID BY ADDRESSEE

READER SERVICE
PO BOX 1341
BUFFALO NY 14240-8571

NO POSTAGE
NECESSARY
IF MAILED
IN THE
UNITED STATES

Chapter 13

Casey felt invigorated as he lay there beside Melody, breathing hard, holding her tightly against his bare skin. He wondered whether they could enjoy each other even more tonight, just in case this was their last night together. Or even if it wasn't.

Melody had attracted him before. She definitely did now. But he realized this was a bad idea, in many ways. So what? It had been one of the most amazing experiences in his life, here in the dim light of the lanterns, where he could see Melody's body, full of curves in all the right places, which had felt even better as he caressed them. And then he'd made love with her.

"I take it you're still awake," Melody said against his shoulder. She felt warm. Very warm, which was more than welcome in the coolness of the tent.

"Yes, and I guess you are, too." He began moving his hands along her bare back, then down, where he could grasp the globes of her small, tight buttocks.

Which made his erection start thickening and hardening once more…

"That was…wonderful," Melody breathed. "But I'm not quite tired enough to sleep, so—"

She didn't have to say any more, especially since her hand moved down between them and touched him and made him want to do anything—everything—but sleep.

He could only breathe heavily and smile as they made love once more.

And then again…

Afterward, Casey just lay there, still—again—holding Melody closely against him, but only after, this time, unfolding the other sleeping bag on top of them for warmth. He figured that was exactly what they would do at last: sleep.

He felt sated…for now, at least. How would he feel in the morning?

In the future?

Well, he'd find out—

He finally felt himself relaxing enough to fall asleep.

He woke up early the next morning, or at least there was a small bit of light seeping into the tent.

Melody was still sleeping. She was naked beside him beneath their thick cover and he tamped down the urge to start something new. As enjoyable as it might be, it would take time.

And they had to start once more on their mission out here on this vast ranch as soon as possible.

But... Melody's breathing was still deep, the sound of it—what else?—a melody in his ears, soft and even and very, very sweet.

He'd particularly noticed her scent before, when they'd merely slept together. Now he wondered how she could continue to smell so wonderful after their ride. She must have brought along some kind of body wash with that addictive floral scent. Although maybe that was her natural aroma. He wouldn't put anything past this determined, self-reliant, skilled—and sexy— woman.

He reveled quietly in how close they were, how her body heat warmed him. He wanted to remember every moment of it, knowing how unlikely it was ever to happen again...except, perhaps, if they did wind up sleeping outside again in this tent for another night or two.

But once they returned to reality, after this difficult adventure was over, that would be that.

He'd hope to see Melody now and then, of course, but despite how much he had enjoyed being with her— especially last night—he still distrusted the idea of any relationship.

Not after what he'd gone through with Georgia.

He startled as Melody moved slightly in his arms, as if she was reading his thoughts. But she only murmured slightly and moved more closely against him, if that was possible.

It was certainly enjoyable...and turned him on once more. Not that he'd do anything about that now.

He gritted his teeth, once more in the throes of recollections he wanted to somehow erase from his mind, but realized he never would.

Georgia. Strange that he'd think about her now— or not so strange. They'd had sex, of course, but never like this. But—

Georgia. He suddenly thought of that charm that they'd found where the fence had been destroyed. A silver charm with a *G* on it. His thoughts had touched on it occasionally since he'd picked it up and taken it to the sheriff's department for analysis, and not just because it was an obscure clue of some kind.

He finally recognized why.

At some point during their planning, he'd heard that Georgia's parents had given her a charm to wear in celebration on their wedding day. The charm he'd found had her initial on it. Could it be the same one?

Not hardly…right?

That would be too much of a coincidence. How could Georgia be involved in this rustling situation?

She couldn't. He must still be asleep somehow for all of this to barge into his mind.

He was clearly thinking too much right now. He had to stop.

Or if he was going to think, he'd rather muse over what he'd done with Melody last night.

And…well, if he couldn't just wake up Melody and share again the wonders of what they'd done—and he couldn't, because of their need for speed that day—it was nevertheless time to wake her up anyway. To get going.

And to stop thinking, especially about what they'd done last night. It couldn't continue, after all. He wouldn't want it to, and neither would Melody .

So…the best way to awaken her, and to start their day? He moved even closer and kissed her on her full, enticing lips.

Foolish? Maybe. But it had the result he wanted.

Her eyes popped open immediately and her arms moved enough to draw him closer, until their kiss deepened enough to stimulate other parts of his body.

But no matter how he felt, or what he wanted, they needed to get on the move right away.

Pulling slightly away, he said, "It's morning. Ready to get back on the trail?"

He felt her stiffen a bit in his arms. Had he hurt her feelings? But they had the same goal in mind, their jobs to perform, and she immediately said, "Absolutely."

Her response, to his dismay and surprise, hurt his feelings a bit. But he just said, "Last one up and dressed has to pass out our water and breakfast treats."

She rolled over quickly and soon stood away from their sleeping-bag bed. He rose as well but couldn't help observing her luscious body in the nude once more, before she could pull on her underwear, jeans, T-shirt and hoodie, then comb her hair and arrange it again into a ponytail.

Which only made him feel worse that they hadn't engaged, just this once more, in a tiny, short bout of sex.

But this was the right thing to do. In moments he would get dressed in his warm clothes for the day, including his sweatshirt…though not before Melody had turned slightly and also observed his bare body, which, of course, reacted to her gaze. He ignored it. They had to get on their way.

"Hey, Cal keeps trying to slow down," Melody called to Casey. It was nine o'clock in the morning, and they'd been riding once more over the grassy, rolling pasture toward the red dots on her GPS that indicated where the cattle were. They set a quicker pace than they had before, as planned. As always, before they'd started out she had checked her GPS app. The cattle would soon reach the hill they'd need to get down, in the direction of a long rural road, or turn sideways. It appeared that Casey and she were making progress in catching up with them, but not a lot.

Whichever route the rustlers decided to take, she and Casey would follow. And, hopefully, catch them soon.

Right now, she was enjoying the bumps and movements of being on horseback, even if it wasn't as fast as she wanted. She continued, "Do you think my horse wants us to spend another night in the tent before we catch up to the cattle?"

She was kidding, of course. Last night had been fantastic. And though sex was a wonderful experience in a relationship, what she had with Casey was *not* a relationship.

"Well, I didn't get the impression that Cal and Witchy did anything different last night from what they'd done before, and I doubt they care what their riders were up to, either." Casey's voice was loud enough to be heard over the sound of hoofbeats on the ground.

"Guess you're right." Melody shot a positive expression toward her fellow cattle seeker—well, criminal hunter—and nodded her head, then laughed. "Oh, well."

"Yep—oh, well," Casey returned.

And that should have been the end of it. Melody wasn't going to say any more on that subject that gripped her mind—and her body—even now. Unless she figured out another way to joke about it. Make it clear that, in her opinion, Casey and she would just remain buddies, as well as professional colleagues.

Still, despite their prior conversations and her own thoughts about it, Melody felt a bit hurt. What they'd had clearly meant little or nothing to the man she was with.

Well, she knew better than to wish otherwise. And she knew far better than to expect anything more, no matter how wonderful she had found it.

Something occurred to her that she could ask about in a casual manner...kind of. At least it might indicate whether Casey, too, thought they could remain friends. "So what should I expect if I'm able to join you and your family for Christmas dinner? I think you said your brother lives in Phoenix, right? Will he be joining us here?" And was he coming here to join his family for Thanksgiving? Melody didn't know what they were doing then. Her invitation was for Christmas, an extra month away.

"Probably. He'll want to see our parents, and maybe even me." Casey's expression looked light when she glanced at him. She gathered his relationship with his twin brother remained close, even though they didn't live in the same town.

"You're sure your parents will be okay with me coming, too?" She gritted her teeth slightly, half expecting him to rescind the invitation.

"Oh, they're always fine when we ask friends and acquaintances to join us for Christmas."

She looked away, feeling ridiculously hurt. She was just a friend or an acquaintance, in his estimation.

That was true, but it still felt painful after what they'd shared. Even so, she wanted to continue the friendly conversation. "So what do your parents think about their sons both being in law enforcement, though different types?" she asked. "I gathered from what you said before that your mother might be happier about it than your father." As she recalled, Casey had said his mother had hoped her sons would also give back to the community.

"Oh, she worries about us. They both do. They're always telling us to be careful."

And so would she, Melody realized, if she was part of their family. Which she wasn't, of course. "So *are* you?"

"How careful can I be out here in the middle of nowhere with you chasing bad guys?"

"I wondered about that," Melody responded. "At least your parents' jobs both sound fairly responsible. I don't envy your dad, though, trying to cure people of cancer. At least there's not much danger involved for either of them—unlike working for the sheriff's department or FBI."

"Yeah, and Everett and I have the same likelihood of running into bloody situations as our dad does, since he performs surgery sometimes. Or at least I occasionally deal with bloodshed in my job—not that I dig into people intentionally, of course, though I sometimes get involved in contentious situations. Or I find…well, you know."

She did know what he meant, but she refused to mention Pierce, either, or how they'd found him. Instead, she said, "Glad I'm a ranch hand. Sure, there's occasionally blood involved, especially when one of our cows gives birth, but fortunately things tend to be fairly calm and blood-free."

She did find it interesting that both twin brothers had wound up in law enforcement, though, with their parents in such different careers.

For the next half hour, they talked often but about neutral topics, not generally their families but sometimes about their education and what they liked, or didn't like, about Cactus Creek.

Melody didn't get into her thoughts about the future, though. She liked Cactus Creek, intended to stay here, but she didn't want to marry again.

Although she would regret not starting a family.

Well, maybe someday, if the right man happened to show up in her life…

Not Casey, though. Not anyone, this soon after what had happened to her.

For now, she was glad when they urged their horses to a faster gait, then had them slow for a short while.

Melody then decided they should stop so the horses could rest and nibble some grass, while she pulled her phone out to check its GPS once more.

Were they getting closer to those red dots? She certainly hoped so—although if the rustlers continued to drive the cattle forward at the same pace as they'd been doing, she and Casey might be somewhat closer but possibly not near enough to catch up with them today after all.

But when she looked at the app, the number of miles between the cattle and them had shrunk.

"Hey!" she said. "I don't think our quarry is moving much at all today."

"Really?" Casey's eyes widened. "How close are we?"

"A lot closer than before. And if we keep our mounts at the speeds we've been going and the cattle don't go any faster, I think we're going to do it."

"Do what? Catch up with them?"

"Exactly."

He hoped so. Damn, how he hoped so.

He wanted to apprehend those thieves—and murderers—more than nearly any other perpetrator he'd ever gone after. Get this situation resolved. Find out if Georgia did have anything to do with it, since he couldn't help suspecting her thanks to the charm. Although it could, of course, be someone else who had the same initial, or had a friend or relative who did.

After they'd remounted and set out again, he dug his heels into Witchy's side just a little to speed up her pace a bit more. And, of course, Cal—and Melody— kept up with him.

But even as he did that, he considered again that resolving these crimes, hopefully in an appropriate way, would end this closeness with Melody.

At least with her joining his family for Christmas dinner, he would see her again. Plus, as he'd already considered, he could stop in and see her at OverHerd Ranch sometimes.

But…well, he'd only been with her for a few days. And nights.

And then there was the closeness they had shared last night…

"Hey," she called from slightly behind him. "Hey, Deputy Sheriff Colton. Looks like you really want to catch those missing cattle fast now." She—rather, Cal—caught up with him and he glanced at the beautiful ranch hand beside him. Her hair, in its ponytail, bounced as she rode this quickly. She looked as excited as he felt.

Okay, it would be a good thing to get this criminal activity dealt with at last.

And after?

After, they'd hopefully wind up being friends, at Christmas and otherwise.

"It's about time we made more progress," he said. "Although—well, I don't want to delay anything, but if we happen to get close late, we won't want to start our capture of the bad guys and saving the cattle till daylight again. Maybe we'll spend another night together." He turned and aimed a quick wink at her.

"Sounds good to me. But only if that's how things work out."

Chapter 14

As Melody rode—silently now, as she wanted to concentrate on their task at hand, which might actually come to an end soon—she checked the GPS on her phone screen again. And again. She was continuing to use its special terrain-depiction feature—though they were far enough out that her reception had become bad at times, and things often blurred. That both annoyed and worried her.

Even at this more-than-moderate speed on horseback, she was aware that Casey kept glancing over toward her. She glanced back, managing to give him a grin now and then before looking back at the phone.

She had already recognized before they took off that morning that the cattle were nearing the end of Over-Herd Ranch, where the rustlers would need to decide whether to head down the hillside toward the road a bit beyond it, or get the herd to veer to one side or the other.

Which would they do?

In her visits to many parts of the ranch property, Melody had never come this far. She didn't believe there was a fence all the way out here to indicate the end of the ranch property, but she wasn't sure.

But for all she knew, there was a fence out here, too, that was slowing the cattle they were chasing. The GPS map did show a line that could just have been the edge of the property, but it might also be a fence. It also indicated rises and drops in the topography, including rocks and, to some degree, bushes and trees.

And not too far in the distance, she could see more underbrush growing, which indicated this part of the pasture either hadn't initially been cleared and replanted as well as the rest, or simply wasn't cared for as well.

Melody still assumed the rustlers would veer off to one side or the other. It was the practical way to go, although where would they head next? Staying somewhere on OverHerd Ranch didn't seem like a good option. Were they neighbors of this property? Maybe that was the answer. They'd drive the stolen cattle onto their property and sell them.

Although if their herd suddenly increased in size thanks to some valuable Angus cows, wouldn't someone notice?

Someone with clout, and money, like Clarence—or someone who'd want to make a good impression on their rich neighbor who happened to be the town selectman?

Or the rustlers, neighbors or not, might just go ahead

and drive the cattle toward that public road, assuming they'd get down the upcoming hillside easily and safely enough. Rather than keep the stolen cattle around here, wasn't it more likely they'd take them somewhere else to care for, or sell?

Had they already changed the brands on all the cows to SG, as they had with poor, dead Addie? And what did it mean?

And speaking of safety, why endanger the valuable stock they'd stolen by potentially getting them hit by cars on the road?

Of course, that assumed there would be vehicles out here in the middle of nowhere on this mild November day.

If that was the decision, surely even the rustlers would want to slow and stop the cattle. Herd them somewhere away from the road. The animals wouldn't be worth anything dead.

And people in vehicles would be at risk, too—not that the rustlers were likely to give a damn about that. They already had one animal death and a human murder on their shoulders.

She was not just OverHerding, she was overthinking this situation, Melody realized. Even so, she continued to view the map on her phone, which she held with one hand while the reins remained in the other. At the moment, that map was fairly clear.

"Hey, it's one thing to keep track of those cattle," Casey called over to her. "But you look like you're going to get bounced right out of the saddle since you're going this speed and not really hanging on. Haven't you checked the location enough?" Cal was keeping up with Witchy, and Casey looked damn good as a cowboy in the saddle even at that speed, his posture straight and his shoulders back. Melody wasn't exactly happy about his criticism, but the idea that Casey was concerned about her safety sent a little pulse of pleasure through her.

And she was, of course, going forward swiftly. Even Cal's long, deep brown mane was blowing erratically in the wind around them, something like her own ponytail.

"Just trying to determine which way they're going." She described the hillside, the road and the possible fence, as well as mentioning the likelihood the rustlers might instead take a sideways route. "I'm not sure which would be best for us, but I'm sure that's not a factor for them." Melody almost laughed at the sound of her own voice as it became sometimes garbled and uneven as she bounced.

Casey didn't complain, though. He did, however, call to her. "Okay, then. Let's slow down a little. We need to come up with a plan to get right up on where they are and bring down the rustlers, whichever way they go."

Sure enough, Witchy started slowing down as Casey pulled slightly at her reins. What else could Melody do but slow Cal as well? She was kind of the law-enforcement assistant here. She couldn't save the cattle and bring down the bad guys herself.

That was more smart and skilled—and good-looking and sexy—Deputy Sheriff Casey's job.

Casey pointed toward what appeared to be a gully off to their side, surrounded by bushes. "Let's let the horses get a drink, okay? We can hopefully purify some water there. I wouldn't mind a drink, too, so I need to get my bottle out of my saddlebag."

What? Actually stop here when they were getting close?

But Melody realized she was thirsty, too.

Besides, not knowing what the rustlers were up to, if she and Casey got too close without a plan, they might somehow be outmaneuvered.

Or even attacked.

Okay, a rest. A drink.

Some discussion.

Hopefully, when they continued forward again they would have more of a plan.

But first…what was that? Something on her screen was changing, and she needed to understand why. Was it because of poor reception? It didn't seem that way. In fact, the reception appeared fairly good here.

Would what had changed at last provide her with the answers they needed?

Casey liked how Melody seemed so dedicated to their task, which he hoped—believed—would come to an end soon. But as much as he wanted to capture the murdering rustlers and bring in the missing cattle, he wanted to do it safely, with Melody at his side, not falling off her horse and getting hurt because she was trying so hard.

And if it wound up taking an extra night, as they'd mentioned before? Well, his body reacted slightly at the very idea, though that wasn't the point.

No, they needed to do things safely and well.

Hence, their break right now. It should be good for their horses, too. And he wouldn't allow it to slow them for long.

He slid off his saddle and helped Melody down— not that she, a skilled ranch hand, couldn't have done it herself. But once again, he was concerned for her safety, partly because she'd just begun really staring at and manipulating the screen on the phone in her hand like some careless teenager glued to something on social media or whatever.

He had seen several situations at the Sur County Sheriff's Department where young people had done something similar while driving and caused accidents. Hurt themselves, and sometimes other people.

Out here, Melody probably couldn't harm anyone but herself, but she wasn't going to do even that if he could help it. And he could.

Besides, touching her even so neutrally felt good.

"Everything okay?" he asked, but she didn't respond. Not yet. But he'd get her to talk to him and let him know what was on her mind.

Soon.

Once she was standing by Cal, still swiping at things on the screen in front of her, Casey returned to Witchy and took his horse's reins, directing her toward the slope down to the small creek running through the middle of some bushes near them. When he'd gotten some water ready for her and his horse seemed happy, he returned to get Cal and make sure Melody knew what he was doing.

She didn't even spare him a glance at first, though

she looked up immediately when he joined her after taking Cal to Witchy's side. "You've got to look at this," she said, gesturing with her phone.

At last. He'd get some answers. "What's going on?" He spoke more firmly this time and fought back an amused urge to inquire whether she'd discovered a new YouTube video. But he had come to know her well enough over the past few days to feel certain that whatever she'd found, it had something to do with their quest for the cattle and the thieves.

Maybe even, considering Melody's apparent excitement, something that would help them end their search at last.

She looked so gorgeous standing there, her dark hair framing just one side of her pretty face since her head was tilted, her deep brown eyes agog with what appeared to be excitement. Although was there just a bit of puzzlement there, too?

Was he coming to know her well enough to read her expressions and know what she was thinking?

He hoped so, but still, he wanted to know what was causing her to apparently nearly bounce up and down on her toes as she continued to stare at her phone, then back at him as she waved it in invitation for him to see, too. She looked so cute behaving like this.

So appealing. Even so, the reason he drew closer was because of what she said.

"I've got to show you this," she told him. "I've been trying to figure it out and have at least a clue, though no real answers yet. Take a look."

She still held the phone, but this time it was in front

of both of them. He bent to touch his shoulder to hers as he looked.

The map he saw this time appeared fairly detailed, with more ups and downs and trees and rocks and bushier plants. It seemed to indicate they were heading into a slightly different environment.

But that wasn't the only thing that was changed. Except for that same poor, dead cow, the rest of the red dots indicating the whereabouts of the missing cattle had previously been clumped together.

Not now.

"I've been watching this for a while," Melody said. "Some of those dots are moving individually. At first, it was just a couple, and then they stopped. And then those couple were joined by one more that had left the first group, which still remained a group. More are apparently being led away the same way, and I think we need to figure out where…and why."

"I agree." Casey looked up and stared in the direction they'd been moving, since that was also where the cows were previously being led, together, in a group.

What did it mean that it appeared they were now being led individually, at least for a short distance? Did that have to do with the topography?

He asked Melody her opinion as he held out his hand to look more closely at her phone. She was better skilled in manipulating the screen and figuring out locations using the GPS, so for the next few minutes he did what he could to look more closely at the dots and the cattle's surroundings—and Melody helped by reclaiming her phone, swiping or otherwise changing it now and then, and handing it back to him.

"So what do you think?" she asked him finally.

"I think we need to get back on the trail, but not as quickly since our quarry seems to be slowing down, whatever it is they're doing."

"That could work out well for us, right?" Melody was looking up at him now, and not at her phone. Her dark eyebrows were lifted and her expression appeared hopeful.

"Guess we'll find out," he told her, nodding as if he fully agreed with her.

He only hoped she was right.

So how were they going to deal with this? It was Casey's call, of course, but Melody wanted to know in advance what they would try.

Best she could tell from her GPS map and those individual, sometimes moving dots, that hill at the end of the ranch property could be steeper than she'd figured, and she explained that to Casey. It did seem to be shrouded in plants, and it overlooked the road that showed up on her map, in the distance.

Whatever it meant, the rustlers had apparently reached that location. Instead of veering right or left, it seemed that they had decided to lead the stock forward, one at a time—possibly down that hillside she speculated about, rather than herd them forward as they'd been doing previously.

"I'd really like to see that area close up, before we

reach the rustlers and cattle," she told Casey. "I don't know what we should expect, at least not exactly."

"Nope, but you're right about needing to get closer to observe and make a rational decision what to do next," Casey said. "And surprisingly, we may be in a good situation for that."

"What do you mean?"

He pointed at the gully where they still stood with the horses and the bushes around them. "Since it's November, some of the plants have lost their leaves but kept their branches, even little twigs, so there's still some substance to them." Then he said, "Let me see your phone, please."

She handed it to him, watching both him and the phone closely to try to determine what was on his mind.

"If you're right about the meaning of the dots in clumps and individually here, about half the cattle have been led down the hill. That means we should get closer soon. We're less likely to be seen if we're on a different level from the rustlers, but we don't know that."

"So what are you thinking?" Judging by the intense expression on his face, she had no doubt he had something on his mind.

"We should probably go just a little farther through these bushes." He waved around them. "Then hitch the horses someplace where they can stay a while. You and I can hurry, under cover as much as possible, to the hilltop and figure out which cattle—and rustlers—are where. Then we can at last go after them."

Chapter 15

This could be interesting, Casey thought as he walked Witchy along. But they were definitely approaching the place where the rustlers were apparently still leading the cows down the hill one by one.

He found himself thinking a lot about what had already happened and what was going on now, rehashing it all in his mind and therefore not talking much, at this point, with Melody.

Pretty Melody. Determined Melody...

He glanced at her and saw that she was studying the terrain ahead of them and off to the right, where hills rose and fell, and bushes abounded. She appeared to be thinking, too.

One of the main things he thought of was the extent of his wondering from the beginning how this entire situation was finally going to end. He'd made himself not dwell much on how to bring the murderous rustlers to justice once they caught up to them, but he intended to improvise strategically and wisely once any opportunity arose. He was generally a planner, but there had been too many unknowns out here to try to zero in on a plan of attack that might be impossible to undertake.

Sure, he had a gun with him, but he didn't know how many people they might be up against. His improvisation might involve Melody, as long as he could keep her safe. Or maybe he would determine it was time to get some backup from the sheriff's department here. A lot was still to be decided, depending on what they found.

Plus he'd remained concerned, out in the vast open-pasture areas, whether Melody and he would be seen on their horses long before they caught up with the cattle and rustlers, and the bad guys would slaughter the cattle and escape themselves. That had always been a major worry, even from the first, when they'd decided to conduct the chase on horseback rather than by all-terrain vehicles or helicopters overhead, and his concern had grown even more intense after they found Pierce's body.

Why had he been killed? Because he'd simply gotten too close? As a warning to others? Both? Or had Pierce actually been involved with the rustlers?

Casey had figured Melody and he would be okay as long as the criminals couldn't actually see their pursuers. And Melody and he weren't wearing GPS trackers, although if the bad guys had the phone information of either of them, they might be vulnerable that way. But surely they didn't have that, especially if they didn't know they were being followed—though they might suspect it, of course.

Still… His life, and Melody's, could be at risk. Probably were. Best he could do was to stay aware and alert and be prepared to do anything necessary to deal with the situation. They would continue following from a distance, finding some kind of cover before they got too close. He'd always intended to observe the rustlers and gather information before calling his department in for backup to help end the situation. But he had to see more of what was going on before that became feasible. And his number-one priority then would be to protect Melody.

One good thing was that he felt sure she'd be glad to wrangle the cattle away and protect them no matter what he was doing. He, as the armed deputy sheriff, could take care of himself. Or call in that backup.

But one way or another, this had to come to an end. A good end for them and their mission.

Most particularly if they could do more than simply point at the rustlers. They would need to prove that the bad guys they found were the thieves and killers.

Would determination of the changed brand on the cattle, SG, help with that, assuming that the dead cow, Addie, wasn't the only one that had been done to?

And that charm that was now being analyzed. Would it help somehow in identifying the killer?

Sure, it was interesting being out here, chasing the stolen cattle. But he was a sheriff's deputy. He needed to ensure as much as possible that there was evidence to bring down the bad guys.

"Are you okay?" Melody said from off to his left. When he glanced over yet again, she wasn't glued to their surroundings or her telephone screen as she rode on Cal's back, but was looking at him.

"Yeah," he said, relieved in a way to move his thoughts to her and engage in a conversation. "I'm just trying to think this through better than before, when we were just following but didn't have a plan in place for stopping the rustlers."

"You have one now?" She sounded excited. "I'd been thinking about that more now, too. A lot more. But I hadn't come up with anything besides continuing to follow, nothing that guaranteed us to come up with the perfect outcome."

"Hey, I want a guarantee," he said facetiously. Then he grew more serious. "And it's kind of you not to give me a hard time for not having it all planned out."

"Of course I wouldn't. We're comrades out here in all ways. I'll help you and expect you to help me, too, depending on how things go. But the main thing…well, I just want this to come out right. No more dead cows." She paused, and Casey looked at her. There were tears on her lovely cheeks as she said, "Or people."

Casey wanted to get them both down off their horses and hug Melody, and not just out of sympathy for her. He hated that another ranch hand had lost his life on his watch. And it had been someone who'd been known by and liked by Melody, which only made the situation worse.

For now, though, he figured they needed to more

fully develop and implement his plan, now that the end was conceivably in sight.

"You're right," he said. "There's been enough blood shed already. Our first priority will be to prevent any more." Okay, he fibbed a little. If he had to shoot or otherwise harm the bad guys to end this, of course he would. And the fact they had already murdered someone suggested they wouldn't be averse to attempting to physically harm Melody or him, either.

He wouldn't allow that.

"Absolutely." The look she shot at him suggested she admired and trusted him, believed in him, figured he'd do his job perfectly as a deputy. He might be reading too much into it, of course, and hoped he did, since the whole idea made him squirm in the saddle.

He was far from perfect. But he would do anything, even give his own life if necessary, to protect her.

Once more, he was overthinking. Sure, he now had a plan. Was it a great one? Probably not, but he would succeed—he had to.

So what was the plan Casey had in mind? Melody really wanted to know.

She'd figured, judging from his expression during the past mile or so as they rode, that he was deep in thought. His thick, light brown eyebrows were furrowed into a pensive frown, even as he continued to look ahead of them and around, as if studying their surroundings for the answers he sought.

No clues out here to help him figure out who the

people were that they were after. Since he was an officer of the law, that was probably on his mind.

Hers, too, in a way. Whoever they were, they'd killed Pierce. Why? Would they try to kill her, too?

And Casey?

Well, she'd been looking around and searching for answers, too, and after a while of not sharing anything but, in effect, their environment, she'd thought it was finally time for her to say something. And so she did.

And, of course, the brief conversation she'd initiated had morphed into something emotional, at least for her.

But she could turn it now into something a lot more useful and, hopefully, more effective.

"So," she said, "it's time. Let's discuss your plan and see how we can best get it implemented." Or possibly not, if she didn't think it made sense.

But she had come to know the man beside her—this deputy sheriff with a conscience and a heart—well enough to believe that, whatever he'd been pondering, it could potentially finish this long, lengthy stakeout in the best way possible. Successfully. It had to be.

"First, can you check your GPS? I could do it, but you're better at it out here than I am. I want to confirm that the cattle still seem to be beneath that hill they were apparently being walked down."

Melody quickly took her phone from her pocket and looked. Again. And she was able to confirm the information for Casey. "It appears that eight of the cattle are in a herd together at the bottom now. Two more may still be at the top of that hill, and another's on the way down, if I'm interpreting this right."

"I'm sure you are."

She glowed a bit under Casey's smile and nod toward her, but stayed quiet, waiting for him to continue.

"Okay. Here's what I'm thinking now." He described a scenario where they'd go a bit farther, getting closer to where the topography dipped downhill, then dismount.

Next, the two of them would advance farther on foot, using more underbrush and the rolling land as their cover while they got nearer to the edge of that hillside, where they should be able to see the rustlers.

"We'll observe them then and figure out the best way of bringing them down...and saving the cattle, of course," he explained. "Does that work for you? Do you have any suggestions? Of course, we can modify anything as we go along, if it seems appropriate."

Fine, Melody thought. But he'd better take good care of himself, too. "It sounds really good in generalities," Melody said. "And, yes, as long as it's all subject to change I'm fine with it. Only—"

"Only you're concerned about our excellent mounts here, aren't you?" Casey leaned forward and stroked Witchy's neck.

"How did you guess I was going to address their welfare further?" Melody was both amused and impressed. It wasn't a surprise, though, that Casey had come to know her well enough to understand how much she liked the livestock in her life.

"A little bird told me. Oh, no, wait. It had to have been a little horsefly." Casey smiled, and Melody couldn't help laughing. "Well, what I figured is that once we get into range of where I think it's time to leave our horses, I'll let you check it out and make the decision as to when and where to tie them up. Securely and safely and with grass and water around, since we're not sure how long they'll have to stay there without us."

Like, would they ever return? Melody wondered that immediately. If all went well, of course they would. But if it didn't, would there be time and opportunity to contact other ranch hands or some of the deputies Casey worked with to ask for their help in saving the horses, too?

Well, the two of them had to do things right so this wouldn't become an issue. Melody knew that and she trusted Casey well enough to believe he'd do everything in his power to make sure not only the cattle, but also these wonderful horses, came out of this situation healthy and happy.

And he'd said he would let her make the decision. "Thanks," she said. "I'm not sure I'll be able to figure out the best locale for the horses so I'll want your input, too, but I appreciate that you'll let me make the decision."

"Oh, I've got a feeling that if I attempted to do it all on my own I'd hear something from you, like it or not."

"You've got me," Melody said with a laugh, and then realized that her words could be interpreted as a bit suggestive.

Well, they'd not get that opportunity now, while finally at the stage of finishing this vital assignment together.

"So after we secure the horses, we'll hike toward where the cattle are, or at least approach the hillside they're being led down?" Melody was fairly certain that was what he'd said and what he intended, but she needed to keep talking now, so she would know what he was thinking. She also wanted to keep her own thoughts in line with what they would need to do, and not be distracted by any unwanted, though much-too-tempting, ideas.

"That's what I think will be best. I'm just hoping there'll be enough bushes or other cover around there so we can continue on foot without being seen. And since we need to do it today, hopefully the cattle won't be too far ahead of us by then."

"There's that road parallel to the base of the slope that's not far away," she reminded him. "I'm hoping the rustlers are smart enough not to attempt to drive the cattle to the other side, at least not if there are any cars at all using it."

"So far, we don't really know how intelligent the criminals are," Casey said. "They can't be too smart since they stole some pretty valuable cows from one of the town's most powerful people. No way would your boss back down and allow them to keep going with any part of his herd."

"And no way would I stop now without making sure those cattle are nice and safe and back with the rest of the herd." She hadn't needed to say that, of course. He knew that.

"Right. And no way would I stop and give up and let those felons escape without my arresting them."

"So we're together on this," Melody said, as if there'd

been any doubt before. But she was enjoying their teasing fellowship at the moment.

"We're together on this," Casey agreed, and the grin he shot her way…well, did he really intend it to look as sexy as it did?

Not that it mattered. Not now, when they were still out chasing their quarry, and not later, even after all had been resolved—favorably to them, she reminded herself. There could be no other result. Period.

"So let's find that right spot for our buddies here," Melody said. She scrutinized the area in front of them.

"Absolutely."

They only continued for about another twenty minutes before Melody said, "Let's stop here and take a look at this place." It was an area where there were lots of bushes with thick branches, as well as a few trees that appeared to be firs. At the far side, the narrow brook they had seen before ran by. There were patches of tall grass, as well.

To Melody, it appeared ideal. "I vote for this location," she told Casey while still seated on Cal's saddle. "If you want to look farther, we can give it a try, but I suspect we'll return here. What do you think?"

He looked ahead of them. From Melody's perspective, the route to the hill dropoff was getting close. She saw no cattle at the top, nor any people to watch them or spot the horses. The last of the cattle must have been accompanied down.

She waited, though, to hear Casey's opinion. He was the law-enforcement agent, after all. In some ways, he was in charge—as long as she didn't disagree with him.

"Let's get down and have a look," he said.

"Good idea."

Melody edged herself out of the saddle and eased down to the ground. She tied the end of Cal's reins to a nearby bush just to make sure he didn't start walking away, and noticed Casey do the same with Witchy.

For the next few minutes, they wandered around the area. It still looked appropriate to Melody but she wanted to hear Casey's opinion.

"I think you're right," he said, and she enjoyed his appreciative smile. "You ready to do a little hiking?"

She considered his question for a moment. "Soon," she said.

She was glad her boots were comfortable and made for walking and more, with their laces tied nice and firmly. Her work shirt and jeans felt just fine in this warm temperature. She'd get warmer, anyway, as they proceeded.

To make sure Cal felt comfortable after they attached him here for his safety, she removed his saddle and saddlebag and placed them on the ground, and also removed the bit from his mouth and loosened his girth. She was happy that Casey did the same with Witchy. Fortunately, the brook appeared fairly clean and they left the horses near enough that they could drink from it. But Melody also left filtered water in containers near both of them.

She then reached inside her saddlebag and removed her fanny pack, making sure it contained her wallet and personal information, which she wouldn't want anyone else to pilfer, as well as some tissues and other things for comfort. She fastened it around her waist.

"I'm ready," she finally said to Casey, who had also been checking his saddlebag on the ground and removing a few things, which he stuck in his pockets.

The last thing she noticed was that he took out his gun and stuck it into the back part of his belt. He wore a long black shirt outside his white T-shirt, with the gun hidden beneath it.

He turned and walked over to her then. To her surprise, he got close. Very close. Close enough that he pulled her into his arms for a tight hug, and, of course, she reciprocated before even considering whether it was a good idea.

And when she looked up at his face, she saw his heated glance back down at her. In moments, their mouths met in a hot kiss. A very passionate kiss. Appropriate out here? Well, why not? She threw herself into it. But it was too brief.

Casey pulled away more quickly than she was ready for, but it was for the best. "I'm ready, too," he said.

Chapter 16

Casey wasn't sure how best to approach the hilltop. Thanks to Melody's GPS, he believed the bad guys had gathered the cattle just beyond the foot of it. Hopefully, they were with the cows now. In any case, there was no sense in being too obvious in his approach to the edge, especially with Melody. He asked her to walk close to the plant life beside them and sometimes even close to the cover of the bushes, where there was room, just in case one of the rustlers sneaked back and checked out the direction from which they'd come for anyone who might be following.

Like them.

If anyone ahead had exceptional hearing, perhaps they'd even be able to make out the crunching of his and Melody's feet on the dead leaves on the ground.

He looked back at his companion often, glad they were both wearing long sleeves since bushes along their route scraped at them constantly. He was also glad they were both dressed in dark colors, to help limit their visibility.

At least the air temperature remained tolerably warm, even though it was now midafternoon.

Melody tapped his shoulder, so he stopped and turned toward her. "Is it okay to talk in a normal voice now?" she asked softly. "Otherwise, you probably won't know I'm saying anything."

He started walking again slowly, beside her. "Should be fine for now, but not when we get much closer. I'm not sure when we're likely to run into anyone, or if they'll be able to hear us from down the hill."

"Our footsteps in the dried leaves of these bushes make a lot of noise, too." She'd noticed that as well, which wasn't surprising.

She was frowning in apparent concern, and he wanted to reassure her all would be well. But he couldn't do that. Not without taking the chance he'd be lying. Instead, he found something to ask her. "Do you know what kinds of plants these are?" He gestured toward the low bushes beside them, then raised his hands to where tree branches stuck out overhead. A few times he'd caught a sweet aroma that originated from the nearby growing things.

"Not really. My thing is livestock, not plant life. But if you wanted me to guess, I think some of these bushes are honeysuckle, or barberry...maybe. And the trees? We've already decided some, those tall ones, are likely to be firs of some kind, and the ones that aren't evergreens might be a type of mesquite, and maybe a type of buckeye."

"Who says you don't know your flora? Don't know if you're right, but that certainly sounds good."

They continued to walk beside each other. Casey had an urge to grab Melody's hand—just to help stabilize her, he told himself.

But she clearly didn't need any assistance to stay upright and move quickly and steadily alongside him. Still, he kept her closest to the cover of the bushes, so she did occasionally reach out to push some greenery, or bare branches, out of her way.

As they inched closer to the top of the hill, Casey developed his plan further. One that would keep Melody safest. He would take all the chances, although he wasn't yet certain how much cover there would be to keep him from being obvious to the bad guys. He couldn't yet see the actual slope beyond the wide summit, although it shouldn't be too bad if the rustlers had managed to get the cows down it, one at a time.

That probably indicated someone standing at the base could see someone leaning over the top, though, or slipping down it some way. But he would nevertheless figure out a way once he was closer to get to the level of the cattle, without being seen.

Depending on what he observed, if he believed it was too dangerous he'd tell Melody to remain in hiding up here.

And somehow find a way to get her to agree. That woman definitely had a mind of her own.

If he could find a way to convince her it was in the

cattle's best interest for her to wait on top of the hill, that might work.

But he preferred not to get killed or captured, either. His gun remained easily reachable, stuck into his belt. And once he saw the actual layout, he would determine the best way to close in on the rustlers.

He would then perfect his plan.

He kept checking the area around them. There did appear to be paths leading sideways into the cover of the bushes and trees, which could be okay. If he found a way to head in that direction and get down the hill beyond the point the rustlers did, he might be able to draw nearer without them seeing him, especially since these bushes and other growth appeared to be fairly thick off to their right.

"Are you trying to figure out how to get down that hill without being seen?" Melody asked even more quietly than before, remaining at his side as he slowed just a bit.

Damn, but she was perceptive. And smart. And... well, attractive. Too attractive, even in her casual clothes out here in the middle of nowhere. Ranch-hand clothes. Not that he hadn't noticed that before. He had to get himself to stop thinking about it, and her, though, and what was beneath those clothes...

Now, especially, when they were reaching the end of their journey, and the possible meeting with the bad guys they were chasing, was a bad time for distractions like that.

Those thoughts were irrelevant to where they were, what they were doing. He had to think deputy-sheriff thoughts only—to accomplish his mission out here, where Melody was simply his colleague.

Or not so simply.

"Yeah," he responded. "I've got some ideas, and I'll welcome any suggestions you have, too."

They talked about it briefly. Melody had some thoughts about going in the other direction from the way he'd been considering, toward the left, maybe until the area at the top of the hill grew level, assuming it eventually did as she'd learned from the GPS, then hurrying to the roadway and walking back that way.

"But I doubt that would work well even if the hill does end in that direction, the way it appears," she said, gazing straight into Casey's eyes. She looked to be even more worried than she had on most of their expedition. "For one thing, I'm not sure what the road shoulder's like. We wouldn't want to walk down the middle of the road, of course. We'd not only probably be seen, but we'd be more likely to get hit by a car."

"My thought was going the other way." Casey pointed off to their right side, into the bushes that were their current cover. "I'd like to head that way before we get too close to the hilltop."

"Will we be able to see what's going on below from there?"

"Don't know yet," he admitted. "We'll just have to check it out. And if that doesn't work, maybe something that will work will become obvious."

"Or not," Melody said glumly. "If not...well, I've been thinking about contacting Clarence and maybe getting him to send a van or two down the road to hopefully collect the cattle there."

"And I'm telling you not to do that," Casey said abruptly. "I don't want any more of your ranch hands put into the line of fire, not till we have some control over what's going on. Besides—" he looked her straight in her beautiful face with an expression he hoped appeared concerned—as well as reminding her who the leader of the two of them was "—your cattle will be endangered more that way, too. If the rustlers see any indication that their prey is about to be collected, they'll most likely start killing all of them, the way we've been afraid of all along. And us, too, if we're close enough and they've noticed us."

Melody shook her head and looked down, walking forward once more. "You're right. But I just don't envision anything coming out the way we want now. I'm glad we've been following and are about to catch up with them, but… Look, I don't want to be critical of you or what you've been doing, but—"

He laughed harshly, feeling as if she'd kicked him where it hurt. Nevertheless, he understood, and acknowledged it.

"You're right," he said. "Our just following was a good idea, before. Now we need to do something to end it. *I* need to do something," he amended. "And…well, I understand why you don't trust me. But I'm damn good at my job." And he was—though he'd never been in this kind of situation before. Even so, he continued, "You need to follow my instructions as we go ahead.

We'll save your cattle and bring down the murderous thieves. I promise. Got it?"

She'd stopped walking again at his outburst, which was a good thing. She seemed to study his face, as if hoping the truth was there.

And then she nodded. "I trust you, Casey," she finally said. As if to punctuate and underscore her words, she stood on her toes, pulled down his neck and gave him a big, hot kiss right on the mouth.

Which made him want to swear he'd do anything she wanted.

"Good" was his somewhat strangled response. "Now, let's go."

She needed to trust Casey, Melody thought. And she did. He seemed sure of himself, at least in some ways. He might not have all the answers yet, but he seemed certain they'd—he'd—figure out a way to end this appropriately: cattle saved, rustlers arrested.

But...well, he kept going, and so did she. He led her not to the edge of the hill, but into the bushes off to the side where a path had been cleared. His muscles flexed beneath his shirt as he moved small branches out of her way.

"Hey, you know, if nothing else maybe we can locate some interesting birds or other animals here in the forest," he said, clearly joking. "And then you can herd them, keep them together right around here while I go ahead and grab the bad guys. Okay?"

"Yeah, sure," she said, enjoying the slight respite. "Maybe some more kestrels, or spotted owls, if you like birds, but I doubt I'll be able to manage their flocks. Maybe rabbits or rats, though. They might have some interest if I find food for them."

But then she turned back to flash a grin at him and gesture for him to follow—as if he wouldn't. It was her own stab at a joke, sort of. This might be a fun exchange, but she was worried.

What was he really thinking? Was he hoping she'd stay out of his way while he performed his job? Was he thinking about how to protect her?

"Right," he said, catching up with her. "You can go look for some rabbit or rat food, and—"

Stopping again, she glared at him. "Cut it out," she said, nearly exploding. "I know what you're doing. And I appreciate it, if I'm right—that you want to protect me while you go finish this. But I'm doing my job, too. You can go get those evil rustlers, and I'll be delighted when you do. But I'll be right with you, taking care of the cattle. Got it?"

"Yeah," he said, his deep, throaty voice a grumble as he glared at her. "But—"

"No *buts*. Let's do it." Yet again, she hurried ahead of him.

When they'd gone maybe a quarter of a mile farther, Melody noticed that the path they were on had another section, one that didn't parallel that hilltop but connected with their path perpendicularly. Since she was the one ahead at the moment, without even asking his opinion, she headed that way. Plenty of plants appeared at the edges—places they could hide as they looked down.

She felt Casey's hand grasp her shoulder. "Hey, wait a minute. Good idea to go that way, but bad idea to do it like this."

"So tell me how."

"I'll show you," he said. "And, yes, you can join me, as long as you're careful and follow my instructions. Got it?"

They'd stopped walking at the edge of that side portion of the path, and Casey looked down at her sternly. In his face, Melody believed she saw that he was not only taking charge, but there was also concern.

"Got it," she said and grabbed his hand. She gazed up earnestly into his handsome but clearly worried face. Okay. Much as she hated to keep admitting it to herself, he was in charge. She knew it and appreciated what appeared to be his caring nature.

She'd go along with his instructions as long as he didn't shut her out, tie her to a tree like the horses or whatever to end her participation.

His hand felt warm and strong in hers. His expression softened somewhat, and she had to prevent herself from reaching up to bring his head down for another kiss.

"Fine, then," he said. "Here's what I'm planning. For both of us."

He expected some argument when he told her he would do it all from now on.

"I'll head toward the end of this part of the path," he said, "then hide and look down at the area below, and, if possible, make my way down this part of the hillside, preferably totally surrounded by brush so I can't be seen." When Melody nodded, he continued, "You'll stay near the top and watch and, if necessary, you can call out the troops."

Casey informed her he would even exchange phones with her so all she'd need to do would be to push a button to call the sheriff's department, request backup and explain why. He knew the number so, if necessary, he could call them, too, on her phone.

Simple enough.

And he was pleased that, though she stared hard at his face in the shadows as he told her his plan, she didn't argue, despite her increasingly angry frown. Would she yell at him when he finished?

Nothing. Silence when he stopped talking. He sighed inside in relief. He'd go ahead. She'd stay safe. End of story, assuming he did apprehend the rustlers and was able to do that before they could injure any more of the cattle.

"Great," he said after a few moments of silence. "So give me your phone, and here's mine." He pulled it from his pocket, allowing himself to once more feel the hardness of the gun stuck into the back of his belt as further reassurance all would be well.

"That sounds reasonable," she said as she exchanged her phone for his, though she checked the GPS first and showed him that the group of red dots below them was not moving. "Or at least this part of it sounds reasonable."

Uh-oh. "What do you mean?"

Surprise, surprise. She didn't like being left behind, even when he again attempted to make it appear that what he was doing was best for the cattle, not just her safety. But he did remind her about what had happened to Pierce, and that the rustlers clearly would have no compunction about killing Casey and her, too. Coming after them both, if they knew there were two of them.

Beyond saying she would do what seemed right, she didn't argue with him. She just glared into his eyes, her expressive, deep brown eyes hardening beneath her long, dark lashes. Her gaze was much icier than he believed he'd ever seen it before.

Which hurt, damn it, even though he shouldn't care what she thought.

He did.

So he pulled her into his arms and held her close. "It'll work out fine this way," he promised her, hoping it wasn't a lie. "You'll see. And you can call my department if there's any sign of trouble. You'll be in charge."

"Right," she said, speaking against his chest. And then she moved back just a little.

Just enough to pull down his head to hers, where they engaged in what was probably the hottest, most emotional kiss they'd shared. Her use of her tongue reminded him of their night of sex, and her holding him tightly against her seemed a hug of utmost caring. And desire.

Which made his body react. Made him want more. A lot more.

That wouldn't happen, though. Not now, and not later when this was all over. Successfully.

And when the kiss was ended, she pulled back again

beneath the tall bushes where they stood and looked at him, those gorgeous eyes of hers moist but intense.

"Now go for it," she said. "Be careful, okay? I'll be watching. If I see anything that looks like trouble, I'll make that call. And if you want me to call, just put your hand up and wave as if you're waving to the cows. That'll be our signal, okay?"

"Okay," he said, grabbing her for another kiss before heading forward.

Sure enough, she stayed behind him.

He kneeled on the ground as he reached the area where this part of the hill finally sloped downward. He looked where the cattle were.

He could make out three people there at the edge of the herd, though they were far enough away he couldn't tell much about them.

There was one of him. And he had one gun.

Hell. He was glad he had Melody as backup and they had a plan for him signaling her.

It was time for him to ease his way through the bushes and head down the hill.

Chapter 17

Melody sat on the hard, leaf-covered ground beneath a healthy-looking bush that gave her plenty of cover. But back here, within the shrubbery, and still a distance from the end of the path that led down the hill, she hardly needed any cover.

She needed finality. A successful close to their stake-out.

Victory by Casey in what he had just set out to do. Safely. With neither of them harmed, certainly not like poor Pierce. And hopefully they would learn why the murderers killed Pierce.

She hadn't needed Casey's reminder about Pierce. She wondered yet again if her fellow ranch hand had worked with the rustlers, which she didn't want to believe, or, more likely, attempted unsuccessfully to face them down.

And as Casey had mentioned, she couldn't help feeling worried that he, or even she, could be hurt, or worse, too.

She had fought any kind of emotion deep inside her—and not so deep—as he had set off away from her, partly bent over, through the underbrush. She'd watched him head away on the bush-shrouded path ahead of her, finding herself staring at his wide-shouldered back in the dark blue shirt, his jeans-covered butt and legs, and his boot-clad feet until he disappeared. She forced herself to stay put. Not follow.

But did she feel comfortable he'd handle it completely successfully on his own? Of course, she hoped so—but she wasn't going to make the assumption he would and could.

And so she kept his phone clutched in her hand as she made herself remain seated, wanting to count the seconds since he'd left her there. She intended to head after him, no matter what he'd told her, once she'd reached a minute. At the most, two.

But to be as safe as possible that she wouldn't catch up with him, she waited maybe five. Even so, she worried that he'd hear her. Sense her presence some other way.

They didn't need to take the time to argue now. And arguing would definitely make noise, perhaps even enough to let their quarry know they were on their way.

Why follow him? Because she intended to protect him, at least somewhat. She would stay way back, just watch, stay safe herself. And call for help immediately if he needed it. Soon, though, it was time for her to get on the move. She stayed alert, listening and watching to the extent she could under this cover of leaves and undergrowth as she moved quickly forward.

Where was Casey now? Had he hurried his way to the bottom of this part of the hill, or had he stopped to try to observe where the people below were and the best way he could approach them without being noticed, until he was close and aimed his gun at them to bring them down?

Or was there something else a skilled deputy like him would do, some other way to capture the criminals with as little risk to himself as possible?

Heck, she thought as she continued to head in the direction he'd gone. If his main goal was to minimize risk to himself, he'd have had her go with him, from the first, to help. Though she wasn't armed, she could make that call to his real backup immediately when he said to.

But he'd still wanted to protect her. Sweet, but impractical. And more dangerous to him. After all, there were also other ways besides aiming a gun that she might have been able to get the bad guys under control.

That thought made her sweep her gaze around for any sign of a nice, large branch she could use as a weapon if she needed to.

Well, she saw nothing in this confined area, and even if there was something she'd hardly be able to drag a big, heavy branch with her. But she'd keep watching for something compact and potentially usable as she continued forward.

Rationally, though, she realized she would be doing this without a weapon.

At least she didn't see any of the rodents she'd teased Casey about before. Insects, though, and worms…but she worked outdoors. She might not love them but she was used to them.

She had recognized that this part of the downward-sloping hillside was long, but she hadn't considered the amount of time it might take for her to reach the bottom, particularly since, though she attempted to be fast, she tried to move as little visible plant life and make as little noise as she could.

Was Casey going even more quickly than she was? She hoped not. She didn't want to catch up with him, but she wanted to be there for him if he needed any assistance, as soon as she could, once he reached the base of the hill.

Casey. They were partners in this challenging enterprise. They had different skills that should meld well together for finally dealing with the killers and retrieving the stolen cattle. Or so Melody believed, although Casey and she hadn't really discussed it. But she trusted that wonderful deputy sheriff.

And they'd been working on at least finding the cattle for days. Nights.

Night. No more nights together with Casey now. She ought to be glad. Oh, she'd enjoyed their time together—their amazing encounter last night. But there were many reasons for their closeness then—partly to distract and support her after the murder of her co-worker.

But she didn't want to think about Pierce now. She wanted to think about Casey.

It had been fun. It had been memorable.

And it had been a one-time wonder.

Still, maybe they'd remain friends and potential colleagues in other ways. She hated the idea of never seeing Casey again after what they'd been through…and what they were likely to go through soon.

She was thinking too much again. She realized it. And yet how could she keep her mind primarily on sneaking down the hill and remaining off Casey's radar and certainly that of the horrible rustlers?

For the next few minutes, she tried to think of something besides Casey. As a ranch hand, she was outside a lot, anyway. Not creeping down hillsides decked with foliage, but out there wrangling cattle.

She hoped she would be doing that again soon. Very soon. With the remaining eleven of the stolen cattle.

Hey. What was that? She stopped moving and just remained where she was, listening.

Cattle, somewhere far ahead of her. Their sweet, soft lowing. She had to be getting close, and fortunately they didn't sound in distress.

But with them, Melody heard voices, too. Must be the thieves. Assuming she heard what she believed she did. It all seemed so hushed at this distance.

Was one of the voices Casey's? Was he with the rustlers now? Had he already arrested them, gotten possession back of the missing cows?

Or…was it something else? *Someone* else? Who was talking?

Was Casey just listening, too?

Or was he participating?

She just stayed still…for now. Trying to decide what to do.

When to move forward.

She couldn't see Casey yet. Wouldn't be able to view his hand signal, even if he gave it.

Not sure where he was, she figured she might not have been able to see a signal from him even if she'd listened and remained at the top of the hill.

Well, she was going to help him, like it or not. At least she would be there to call in his real backup if he got into trouble.

Their backs were toward him—all three of them. They all wore jeans and thick, full hoodies, as well as tennis shoes, and somehow they appeared nearly the same height that way, though maybe that was because where they stood was somewhat rough.

They were still too far away for him to hear what they were saying, even though it was loud enough that Casey knew they were having a conversation. About the lowing cattle, whose moos helped to obliterate the people's words, that they stood near?

He gathered that was the case, since the few words he made out included "forward" and "keep going."

He had nearly reached the end of the foliage-strewn path and was still hidden within the underbrush, as he intended. Of course, since the perpetrators were looking in the other direction, they might not have seen him, anyway, or any movement he had caused in the foliage.

Damn, but this was frustrating. He wanted to get near enough to at least hear what they were saying, figure out what their plan was, if any.

And then turn his own rough outline of a plan into reality.

Were they all armed? One had shot Pierce. He couldn't assume the others weren't carrying, too. Therefore, what he really would like to do—just dash out there, gun drawn—wasn't a great idea.

Besides, he didn't really want to shoot them, even if they all charged him. He wanted to bring them in, if possible—healthy and whole and able to stand trial. And if they ran away, he definitely didn't want to shoot them in their backs, but how would he stop them? Plus they might all go in different directions, so he would only be able to follow one.

The worst scenario, and perhaps the most likely, was that they'd all go hide among the cattle, in which case there was no way Casey could fire his gun at all.

At least he'd found them, and they remained in one spot for now. This was probably the time to pull Melody's phone from his pocket and call in his backup, though talking here, even softly over the phone, might give him away. He could, instead, reach up and send the signal he and Melody had planned to her. But would she, at the top of the hill, be able to see him?

Would the rustlers see him instead?

What had he been expecting? Something like this, of course. And what was he going to do about it?

Confront them soon. He had to.

First, though, he'd—

He heard some rustling of the undergrowth behind him and pivoted abruptly. Was there a fourth one who—?

Damn. He saw Melody appear at the top of the portion of the path visible to him in the thick foliage. She put a finger to her lips to shush him, as if he'd call out to scold her the way he wanted to, but would then give away their presence.

Without exchanging anything but a challenging look from her and an angry look from him, she sat down on the ground in the middle of the surrounding bushes, pulled out his phone and pressed the button as he'd shown her.

Damn. She surely was aware of the danger they both were in. Scolding was only part of what he wanted to do, like force her back up the hill. Fast.

Was she going to give them away?

Maybe, but he hadn't come up with anything better.

He barely heard her as she whispered into the phone. If all went as planned, she was speaking with Sheriff Krester, telling him where they were and why, and asking for some support to be sent.

That part was good…he hoped. But he turned back quickly toward the view he'd had before.

The suspects remained in the same location, still talking to one another. No indication, fortunately, that they'd heard anything or were worried.

Ah, but Casey intended to change that as soon as possible. But what was the best way to handle things now?

To go back a few feet, where Melody stood, and just

wait there with her…after confirming she'd been told help was on the way?

To move forward, gun in hand, and attempt to make sure the bad guys didn't try anything, like getting away?

Although it wasn't his favorite of the available choices, Casey decided to head toward Melody. If he just ran out there and made noises and attempted to scare the rustlers into submission, he doubted they'd accept that, anyway.

And if that was his choice, he had no doubt that Melody would follow him and put herself into further danger. She'd promised not to, sure. She had also promised not to follow him here or do anything except what he told her.

Well, that was an exaggeration. Which gave him all the more reason to inch his way back to where she was.

She wasn't too far from where he had stopped. His phone was in her hand, and, waving it in front of her, she remained grinning, as if she'd done exactly as he'd told her to.

No…as if she'd done exactly as she'd chosen to, which of course was the case.

He wanted to throttle her.

No, he wanted to kiss those lips that were drawn into such a challenging, sexy smile.

Definitely not here, though. Not now. But maybe a kiss in celebration once they were successful…

He'd have to consider that later, when they actually *were* successful.

For now, he quickly squatted down beside her. Though chastising her wouldn't help a thing right now, he wanted to attempt once more to make her understand that she had to listen to him, to do as he said, to keep herself safe.

"You're supposed to still be at the top of the hill," he whispered so softly that what he said couldn't be any louder than a breeze through the foliage around here. Or at least that was his attempt.

"Then I wouldn't have been able to make that call for you, since I couldn't see you before." She, too, didn't sound any louder than the softest of winds. She'd been slightly louder on the phone, but not much—and that had undoubtedly been of necessity, to make sure the sheriff could hear her.

"Help on the way?" he asked her, even though she'd nodded at him after the call, which seemed to indicate all was well.

She nodded again.

"Okay, then. Let's wait here."

He hated the idea of remaining idle, not doing anything but hanging out until they knew backup from his department had arrived.

Still, it'd be safer for both of them. He could stay here with Melody to make sure she didn't do anything stupid, like run out there and try to protect the cattle. They might not even need protection. Not now, at least. No one was getting them to move anywhere at the moment.

And so he sat down right beside Melody. Close enough so their shoulders touched.

She looked at him, and he had an urge for more than their shoulders to touch—but that was old news.

New news would come when all was taken care of here.

He wanted to know when that would be. He had an urge to return to where he'd been observing the rustlers a few feet ahead of where they were now and just watch. But if he did that, Melody would likely join him, and that was a bad idea.

He kept looking there, though…and the smart ranch hand beside him apparently read his thoughts. "If you want to go keep an eye on things now, go ahead," she whispered. "I'll stay here."

He glanced back at her, and she nodded as if to reassure him she wasn't kidding. Of course, that might be her intention for this moment. For the next…?

Well, he'd take his chances…to some extent. He'd go take a look while keeping an eye on Melody, too.

He nodded his thanks, then took her hand in his and squeezed it—for her reassurance, he told himself. But it also helped his own.

This woman made him want to do everything right now and the right way, for her as well as for himself. She was so different from other women he'd known. She put herself out there, into danger, to help not only him, but the animals she cared about.

After one final squeeze, he reluctantly let go, then edged his way back to where he'd been.

Which turned out to be a damn good thing. He heard one of the people standing there speaking a bit more loudly over the continued lowing of the cattle. "Okay, let's mount up and move them out."

Hell, no. Not now.

Instinctively, Casey drew the gun from where it was hooked on his belt, behind his back.

"What—?" It was Melody, still in a low voice but higher than a whisper.

He turned slightly, and only for a moment. "They're going to herd them again," he said, also slightly louder. "I've got to stop them."

But when he reached the end of the cover provided by the bushes, he stopped.

One of the rustlers had turned sideways enough that he could see her face.

Her face. It was oval and pretty, with sharp features and surrounded by mid-length dark hair. And it suddenly came to him that she actually had received the charm her family had been talking about prior to their nonmarriage. The charm Melody and he had found. The *G*.

G as in Georgia.

His ex-fiancée, the woman who'd snubbed him at the altar—she was involved in this.

Very involved.

Chapter 18

What was going on? Why had Casey stopped?

Had he decided it was too dangerous to continue?

Damn, but Melody wished now that she had a gun. Their backup might be on the way, but for the moment she was the only support Casey had.

And for the moment, though she was watching his back from a short distance behind him and wanted more than anything to do what he needed from her, she had no idea what to do to help.

She felt a vibration in her pocket. Casey's phone. Thank heavens he'd turned off the ringer...although she wasn't surprised. That deputy knew what he was doing in so many ways...

She pulled out the phone and looked at the name on

the screen. The sheriff. Were he and his men here, or at least close?

Again speaking so quietly that she hopefully couldn't be overheard, she said, "Hello, Sheriff. Are you—?"

"You need to apologize to Casey and tell him to stand down for now," he interrupted. "We had an emergency here in town—an armed robbery at a clothing store. A lot of personnel are working on it, but we'll get someone to you soon as we can."

"This is becoming an emergency, too," she sputtered at him, though she still kept her voice low.

"Sorry," he repeated. "You and Casey had better be careful. There's something I may try here to get to you sooner, but not sure how long it'll take." And then he was gone.

Melody hadn't lied. Far from it. This was close to becoming an emergency now. Casey had just stepped out from his cover and into the clearing.

What was he doing? She'd figured there was a problem a moment ago when he'd stopped moving, but this surely was a lot worse. She had to tell him that their backup wasn't yet on the way, and the timing was uncertain.

And for now, she definitely had to become his backup. But how?

Once more she wished she'd brought some kind of weapon, preferably a gun. She'd practiced on shooting ranges. She was a ranch hand, after all.

But she'd never acquired a gun herself.

She heard more talking now. Raised voices. Damn! She definitely recognized Casey's among them, and she could no longer see his back. He must be confronting the rustlers, and he couldn't know how bad an idea that was at the moment.

But even if the sheriff was sending some kind of backup now, Melody couldn't imagine any way Casey could end this himself without anyone getting hurt. Without cattle getting hurt.

Worst of all, without *him* getting hurt.

She had to at least observe, and hopefully come up with a way to keep him safe. Maybe some kind of distraction with the cattle.

Yes, that had to be it…she hoped. To figure out what to do and how to do it, she inched forward to the break in the foliage where Casey had just stepped out to look out at what was happening, who was there and where they all stood, and what Casey was doing.

She stopped when she saw something that startled her and made her stand still.

And listen to the yelling, which continued.

The three rustlers consisted of two women and one man, and they were confronting Casey.

Melody was close enough now to hear what they were saying, despite the somewhat distressed mooing of the cattle that were now just behind the people who faced down Casey. Were the cows upset because of the raised human voices?

The rustlers' horses stood off to the side of the small herd of cattle.

And it became clear to Melody nearly immediately how furious Casey was. He was shouting at the people as if he knew them. "You're such fools," he was yelling.

"Murderers—Sean, and Georgia and even Delilah. So stupid, all of you. Damn you for starting this, and for killing that ranch hand."

He'd drawn his gun, but it wasn't aimed at any of them, at least not at that moment.

But his shouting or insulting or whatever it was had now apparently escalated the argument even more.

Because the man drew a gun and pointed it straight at Casey's chest.

"Why the hell are you the one who's after us?" demanded the assailant holding the gun on Casey.

And why the hell was Sean Dodd, the man who'd helped to steal the cattle, aiming at him? Sean was his brother's one-time best friend and his ex's brother. Casey might not have been overly fond of Sean, even when Georgia and he were engaged, but he hadn't foreseen he'd become a cattle rustler—and a murderer.

Georgia, who stood slightly behind Sean now, was clearly using her brother as a shield to confront Casey.

Georgia, the too-pretty woman with long, dark hair and full lips that had tantalized him once upon a time. The bitch who had left him at the altar…and had apparently dropped that charm near the broken fence, the charm Casey now assumed was hers.

As with her brother, Casey was surprised. Whatever Georgia used to be, he'd also never considered that she would steal cattle, let alone murder someone.

Georgia, who kept peeking around Sean and grinning at Casey so evilly and challengingly that he was tempted to ignore Sean's gun and go confront her, face-to-face.

But, of course, he knew better than to move, at least for the moment. Sure, he still held his gun, too, but he'd stopped himself from pointing and shooting once he was certain who the suspects—more than suspects—happened to be.

People he knew, even if he hadn't trusted or liked them for a long time. Not even the third member of their party, Sean's wife, Delilah. She was attractive, sure, and wore her black hair pulled back to show off her usual dangling earrings and wide-eyed, pretty face that nevertheless seemed intelligent, as an accountant should be. But was Delilah?

What was she doing out here? Was she involved in stealing the cattle, too? It certainly appeared so, but she'd always struck Casey as a nice, normal person.

Why she'd ever married a jerk like Sean was a mystery to Casey. Not that the answer mattered in the scheme of things, particularly here.

And why the heck were any of them rustling cattle, let alone killing people? Why break the law at all? Were they somehow out of money? Doing it just for fun? It must all be new, since he'd had no indication of their being criminals when Georgia and he were together.

Casey kept his tone as mild as possible when he responded to Sean's question, which hung in the air.

"As you're aware, Sean, I'm a deputy sheriff here in Sur County. It shouldn't be surprising to you that I'm attempting to bring down people who are breaking the law. I'd no idea it was you and don't believe anyone else in my department did, either." He paused. "Not that I'm particularly surprised about you or dear Georgia, and since you're involved I guess I shouldn't be surprised about Delilah, either." He stared at Sean's wife, who stood behind the other two looking off to her side…as if she wanted to be anyplace but there.

Maybe. That could, of course, just be his interpretation, or her ruse.

"Well, I'm not surprised, but I'm also not thrilled," Sean said. The guy looked relaxed despite holding a gun on Casey. His hair was brushed high to reveal his long forehead, and he'd grown a scruffy beard since Casey had seen him last. And when Sean smiled, like now, he revealed even, white teeth. "I'd figured we'd just take these cows and sell them and that would be that. Changed their brand so no one would know where they came from, to SG—Sean-Georgia. Didn't really want an escort."

"Oh, you don't have an escort, believe me," Casey said, taking a step closer but still not raising his gun, figuring that would only cause Sean to shoot him. At least Sean hadn't ordered him to drop it yet. And when he did, would Casey obey? He doubted it. "Now, why don't we wind this down?" Casey continued. "You can go back to town, and I'll get the cattle taken care of."

Sean laughed. Sarcasm coated his words as he quipped, "And then I'll take over the town from Selectman Edison and make a little money that way. Hah, hah. As if." His expression changed from a smile to an angry glare. "Forget that. And I—" He looked over Casey's shoulder, and that expression changed again, to…what? Puzzlement? Or was it a smug look? "Hey, I guess I've found a way to end this stalemate, to make sure you do exactly as I say."

What the hell? Casey had a bad feeling, considering the direction of Sean's gaze, that maybe Melody had stepped out from her hiding place. He didn't turn to look. Maybe, even if Melody had been made, Casey could take control while Sean was distracted by having seen her.

"Hey, come out of there, miss," Sean called. "Melody, isn't it? I did a little bit of research before we adopted those cows, and I learned who worked at the ranch, who Edison's ranch hands were. So, Melody Hayworth, why don't you join us?"

Casey didn't hear anything from behind him. Was Melody still hiding? He hoped so. Better yet, maybe she'd started sneaking her way back up the hill. After all, thanks to her, help was on the way. She didn't need to do anything else.

Apparently Sean didn't see or hear more, either.

"Where is she?" demanded Georgia. "Want me to go get her?"

"No need," Sean told his sister. "I can get her to join us, I'm sure." He raised the gun he held a little more, now aiming it at Casey's head. Casey had an urge to duck and roll up to Sean's feet and pull him to the ground. Anything to help Melody. But when Sean yelled out, "I'm about to shoot Deputy Colton here in the head unless you come out here right away, Melody."

"Stay there!" Casey yelled, still not taking his eyes off Sean. Worst case—he hoped—was that he could save himself the same way, by throwing himself to the ground and shooting Sean.

"Ah, at last," Sean said, though he didn't lower the gun. "So come over here, Ms. Ranch Hand."

Damn. Melody must have walked away from the cover of the bushes. And Casey knew it for certain when he heard some footsteps on the turf behind him, and Melody showed up at his side.

He turned slightly to glare at her, but what was the use? Showing anger at her now wouldn't help either of them.

And the half-defiant, half-petrified expression on her face made him want to grab her and hold her and somehow protect her with his body.

Which wouldn't work, if Sean decided to shoot him. Unfortunately, he wasn't made of armor.

"Hello, Casey." Her tone sounded calm and not scared in the least. "And hi to you, robbers." She didn't mention they were killers, too, as she turned to face them, probably a good thing at this moment. "Guess we're at a standoff here. That's a shame."

Casey wished there was a way to ask her if she knew how far away their backup was.

Better yet, he wished the deputies Sheriff Krester had sent would finally arrive.

How long would it be before help got here?

Damn. Melody wasn't surprised that the guy with the gun—Sean, wasn't it? That was what Casey had called him—had noticed her, even though she'd tried to stay hidden. But she had also wanted to watch what was going on with Casey, so she obviously hadn't remained hidden enough.

She wished she could tell Casey the truth about their possibly nonexistent, or at a minimum delayed, backup. But there was no way she could mention it now. And how would his knowing help them, anyway?

The best thing would most likely be to get these people talking, hopefully more relaxed, and just pray that the sheriff got whatever help he'd hinted at on its way. Fast.

She drew slightly closer to Casey, who remained standing with his gun still in his hand but aiming downward. She figured that if he moved it, Sean would shoot them.

She looked then at the two women. Who were they? Georgia and Delilah, Casey had called them. Was Georgia the ex-fiancée he had been talking about? Would there be any way of appealing to them to get their apparent buddy to back off?

First, though, she had a genuine question. "You were right that I'm a ranch hand," she said, directing her gaze back to Sean. "Could you tell me why you stole the cattle?"

"Money, of course," Sean said, sounding almost gleeful. "Your boss knows how to breed some nice, valuable cows. We—" he gestured to the women near him "—need quick cash, so we figured some of Edison's cattle would do the trick."

"And that was your idea?" she asked, even though whose idea it was didn't really matter.

"No, it was mine," said one of the two women as

she moved from behind Sean to beside him on his left side—as his right hand still held the gun. "I'm Georgia." Melody was more convinced now that this was the same Georgia who'd dumped Casey when they were about to get married, especially when she sent a really nasty smile in Casey's direction.

Melody studied her. What had Casey seen in her?

Well, she was somewhat pretty. Besides, hadn't he mentioned that the woman who dumped him had been his childhood sweetheart? So he probably hadn't known then that she was a potential thief—and killer.

Georgia continued talking. "We've heard those Angus cows bring in bunches of money from other ranchers since they have lots of calves before they become expensive and delicious meat. That's why we gave them a new brand. But now that word's out about their theft, we decided to sell them to a slaughterhouse that wouldn't pay attention to even their new brand and would give us a lot of money for them. We'd hoped to do all of it before anyone even knew they were missing. And we certainly didn't take a lot of them. A dozen, from Mr. Edison's huge herd? Why was he even paying attention?"

Melody stifled an urge to go swat the nasty, less-than-intelligent thief right in her grinning face. "Because they are *his*," she said with her teeth clenched. "And they're valuable, as you said. And no one has any right to steal them."

"Oh, we have any right we want," Sean said in a way so offhanded that Melody wished she had a way to swat him, too, without any of them harming her… or Casey, of course.

But what were they going to do now?

"Look," Casey said, "we've got a kind of standoff here. Like I said before, why don't we just end it? You can go your way and we'll go ours—with the cattle, of course."

"Oh, there are a few other options," Sean said. "Like we could shoot you right here and then continue with the cattle."

"Continue where?" Melody asked. "The ranchers around here will all know these cattle have been stolen. Local slaughterhouses, too. No one will buy them now, no matter what your prior plan was." She moved closer once more to Casey, who'd started to ease slightly forward. Why? To grab the gun from that nasty Sean? That wouldn't work.

The guy had already killed one person during this fiasco of a theft, presuming it was Sean who'd murdered Pierce. He definitely had a gun, although she couldn't be certain neither of the women had one. Maybe one of them had done the killing.

And the two who hadn't done the shooting were still accomplices in Pierce's murder, right?

"Oh, we're just waiting now," Georgia responded. "There's a road just ahead, or are you aware of that? No matter. We've got a couple of big trucks on the way to pick the cattle up, move them…well, I won't tell you where."

"Fine," Casey said. "Go ahead. You can just leave us here, and—"

"And you'll find a way to notify your damn sheriff's department and they'll stop the trucks," Sean hissed. "I don't think so—not with you alive, at least." He hadn't moved the gun away from Casey, and now he took another step toward him.

"Now wait," Melody said, attempting not to sound as desperate as she felt. "If you promise not to hurt us, maybe I can help you. As you know, I'm a ranch hand, and—"

"A useless ranch bitch, that's what you are," Georgia said, sneering at her. "Yeah, I'll just bet that you could help. That you would help."

Useless ranch bitch? Melody found herself breathing harder. That insult reminded her of her ex-husband's insults.

Melody's first impulse was to insult this cattle-rustling bitch in return. These thieves facing them down—including Georgia—clearly weren't particularly bright, if they'd thought they would get away with it. Plus they were horrible—cruel to the cattle they were rushing off like this. And atrociously heartless. They hadn't just killed a cow.

They had also killed a man.

Which indicated they wouldn't have any qualms about killing Casey and her, too.

So, though Melody felt she had to say something, it couldn't be anything that would increase the tension in this situation any further.

After pondering for a second or two, she said to Casey's ex, "I do know how to handle cattle." She wondered how he must be feeling to have this particular woman face him down in this situation as a definite enemy. Melody had hated her final confrontation with

Travis, but at least it had been calm despite being nasty. "Let me help you, and I'll—"

"You can help us by shutting up," Sean said, now pointing his gun toward her.

Which she did, even as she grabbed Casey's arm to make sure he didn't attempt to protect her in some way and get hurt.

She nodded, then puckered her mouth to show she wasn't speaking any more, even as she held onto Casey even harder to keep him from talking, too. And she felt him straining at her grasp.

What was he intending to do?

Chapter 19

Damn it all. If Casey had a choice right now, he'd throw his arms around Melody and escort her back into the underbrush to hide, then turn around and confront the deadly idiot standing on the grassy rise just ahead with his gun pointed toward them.

But if he tried it, Casey felt certain Sean would simply shoot him in the back.

Sean. Casey had known the SOB for a long time. He might not have been the smartest tool in the shed then, but he hadn't seemed the type to turn into a criminal.

But who knew? Casey clearly hadn't been particularly discriminating back then, or even afterward. He'd become engaged to Georgia, hadn't he?

Georgia. There was no love lost between them now,

that was for certain. Still, would she want to see Casey killed, especially by her own brother?

Or would she be thrilled about it?

Maybe he should sound her out.

At least the cattle had settled down a bit now behind Sean and the others, maybe because none of the humans were yelling at each other, at least not at the moment.

"So what's this really about, Georgia?" he asked. He looked at his ex as if they were sitting across from each other at a restaurant having a serious discussion, rather than out here, opponents in a standoff, on opposite sides of the law. Both wore casual, outdoor clothing to keep them comfortable in the cooling November climate as evening approached, but Casey felt anything but comfortable talking to her. "Would you have stolen the cattle if you'd known I'd be the deputy to come after you?"

She shrugged her shoulders beneath her hoodie and sent a wry look his way. The prettiness that had impressed him once now just looked plastered-on, a facade. Behind her, the cattle moved restlessly on the grassy, rolling turf under the cloud-strewn sky but fortunately weren't going far, so no one needed to go wrangle them at the moment. Georgia had said they would soon be loaded into trucks that were on their way.

"I didn't know you would be after me," Georgia said. "And I didn't know you wouldn't. It simply didn't matter. We need money. I did what I had to do to get it the fastest way possible. And besides, this has worked before."

"Really? This isn't the first time you've stolen cattle?" Casey was surprised. Sure, the sheriff's department had been involved in similar past investigations of other cattle that had disappeared, but not as many as this time, and not as valuable…and not owned by the town selectman.

Georgia just shrugged, which provided the answer Casey sought. He wanted to keep her conversing with him, though. The more time they ate up in nondangerous dealings, the better chance they had to keep things sort of calm until backup arrived.

How far away were they? Enough time had passed that they should be arriving soon, right?

"Well, did you get money before? How do you think you'll get any from this situation? You'll have a lot of legal charges pending against you, and they won't only consist of grand theft of the cattle. I don't know which of you did it, but one of you shot and killed Pierce Tostig—and that's first-degree murder for all of you."

Delilah suddenly moved in front of Georgia. "I had nothing to do with that," she asserted. "I'm just in this partly because I'm married to Sean, and I do love him, but I'm mostly here because I'm an accountant."

"Then you cooked the family books," Casey said, shaking his head at her.

"Well… I do derive income from my own accounting business, and of course we file taxes, and—"

"I get it." Casey figured he'd enjoy letting the IRS know about that, too—not that it would matter much, when this family wound up in prison, hopefully for life. They'd need to spend any money they had on lawyers. Their tax bill would just be another cost they'd have to deal with.

Interesting that Delilah made no attempt to distance herself from the cattle-rustling situation, but claimed, at least, that she hadn't been involved in the murder. Which she was, just by being with those who'd committed it.

"Yeah, I'm sure you do get it, Casey, dear," Georgia said, this time shuffling in the grass to move in front of her sister-in-law. "But look. I'm sure that, as a mere deputy sheriff, you've got to understand what it's like to need money. We're just—"

"You're just committing crimes, for whatever reason," Casey responded, not attempting to hide his disgust. "You know, I was pretty upset at first when you dumped me just when we were about to get married. And back then, you said it was because your wonderful brother here—" he gestured toward Sean with his empty left hand "—didn't think a mere deputy sheriff was good enough. I wasn't even as good as an FBI agent like Everett, who had no interest in you. I admit I felt hurt. Really hurt. But now? All I can do is thank you. I'm really happy I never married you—not a thieving, murderous person like you."

"Why, you—" Georgia seemed to dive for her brother's gun, but Sean pulled it back, laughing.

"Easy now, little sister," he said. "Let's not do anything hasty. Although I have given this some thought. I haven't come up with any good answers about how best to end this, with this deputy sheriff—" he said the words in a mocking tone "—and ranch hand in a way that won't involve my shooting both of you." He raised his gun hand again slightly. "At least if I do, I can say it was all in self-defense, since you have a gun, too."

In response, Casey lifted his empty left hand as if attempting to wave off the threat, keeping his right hand, which held his gun, still pointed at the ground.

"Look," he said. "Let's be reasonable. I know I shouldn't tell you this since I'd rather you be apprehended right here and now, but I'd suggest you just let us go and get out of here. We've already called for backup, and they're on their way. They should arrive at any time."

He saw Melody ease beside him and felt her touch his left arm. What was she trying to tell him?

Was help not on the way after all?

He didn't dare look at her. He needed to keep his attention riveted on Sean and the women who were his backup.

"Really?" Sean raised the gun higher and aimed at Casey's head. "I bet you're lying. And if you're not... well, yeah, maybe I'll let you stay alive now, as our hostages."

"Well, that's certainly better than the alternative," Casey said, attempting to joke. "And sure, if I thought it would convince you not to hurt us, I'd lie. But I'm not lying. And do you really want to take that chance?"

Casey did manage a quick glance toward Melody, at his side. Her lovely face looked pale and drawn, but she nodded as if in agreement with him.

No, he wasn't lying. Last he'd heard, they did have reinforcements coming thanks to Melody's conversation with his boss, the sheriff.

But she'd had time by herself to talk to Sheriff Krester again. She surely wouldn't have told him to call off their backup. But had the sheriff told her they weren't coming?

Casey had come to know Melody a bit in their few days together, believed he could read her thoughts at least somewhat from her face.

And what he read there right now made him worry. A lot.

Okay, Melody thought. What should she do now?

Telling the truth, the way she understood it, certainly wasn't an option.

Right now, though, she was getting even more terrified of Sean's keeping his gun aimed toward them— especially Casey. They apparently had a history that might even make Sean happy to kill the man who'd nearly become his brother-in-law.

She had to do something. Something to protect both of them. As a member of the sheriff's department, and a guy the people confronting them knew and considered a likely enemy, Casey particularly needed that protection. But what?

She decided to follow through with something she'd suggested before, if nothing else to buy a little time while they talked about it.

Which could wind up being very little time.

"Look, Sean. Georgia. And Delilah, too. You indicated some trucks would be coming down that road soon." She pointed in the direction at the far end of where the cows stood. "I hate the idea of your stealing the cattle that way, but under these circumstances I'd rather you not hurt them while you're loading them up. Let me help you."

"We did okay getting them here," Georgia countered, frowning.

"Except for the one that broke her leg that you then shot." Maybe Melody shouldn't remind them of that, especially in the enraged but muted tone of voice she used. But at least she didn't mention their also killing Pierce.

"Yeah, I think it's a good idea for you to have Melody's help," Casey said. "She knows what she's doing with cattle. And...well, I'd really like to know why you shot poor Pierce." Casey apparently had no qualms about mentioning it, though, she realized.

Melody waited tensely for their response.

"Because he'd caught up with us," Georgia growled, walking slightly down the small ridge where the three of them stood to confront Casey. "Before you did. He threatened us. He was armed, too—and he threatened to shoot us as soon as he confronted us. He seemed so angry about that dead cow, said we'd better give up right away, aimed at us...so Sean shot him."

So now they knew which one was the actual killer, Melody thought. She assumed they now had Pierce's weapon, too, although she didn't want to ask, didn't want to call attention to the likelihood they had at least a second gun among them somewhere.

"I see" was all she said. "Now when are those trucks supposed to get here to pick up the cattle?"

Maybe they could somehow recruit the drivers to help them, depending on how and where they arrived.

She didn't want to get into a situation where other innocent parties, like those drivers, were hurt or killed. Assuming, of course, they were innocent. They might have knowledge of the origin of these cattle, considering the fact they were picking them up in the middle of nowhere.

Behind Sean and Georgia, Delilah was the one to look down at her watch. "In about twenty minutes," she called. Apparently Sean's wife was the most organized, possibly most intelligent one of them. Maybe, if Melody could start walking among them, she could get accountant Delilah to see reality and help her bring down Sean and Georgia—to potentially save their lives, she'd tell Delilah. Otherwise, the people coming as their backup might shoot first before attempting to arrest the armed thieves.

"Okay, then." She glanced around until her eyes lit on the three horses off to the side of the cattle. "Now, as you know, I don't have a horse right here, and herding cattle is easier when you're mounted. Can I borrow one of your horses?" They hadn't agreed she could help them, but they hadn't said she couldn't, either. She might as well act as if it was now a deal.

"What, and gallop away whenever a distraction takes our eyes off you? I don't think so." Sean sneered.

"Besides," Georgia said, "aren't you a big-deal cattle drover? If so, you should be able to get them to go in any direction you want, just by waving your arms and calling to them."

Melody had in fact considered the possibility of racing off as soon as she could, but she'd have been too worried about Casey to try it. She wouldn't tell them that, though. Or Casey. He'd been trying hard to protect her but might resent it if he thought she was further jeopardizing herself to protect him.

"All right, if that's how you want it," she said. "I'd be more help to you if I could be on a horse but I can handle it this way, too. I might wind up giving you more instructions, though, since I won't be able to handle as much myself."

"Oh, yeah, as if we'd follow your instructions," Georgia scoffed.

Melody just shrugged. She'd do what she could to help the cattle—and Casey, too, of course. She would also see what happened when the trucks actually arrived and she had an opportunity to see the drivers and maybe talk with them, and at least show them in some manner what was going on so they'd call for help without Sean and his gang seeing them.

This was it, she realized. Whatever happened in the next hour or less would most likely be the end of this story, and she really hoped she would be able to do something to bring down these miserable rustlers and save Casey and herself…and, of course, the cattle.

There appeared to be no doubt about what the clues they'd found meant. The charm with a G must have been Georgia's. The change in brand on Addie, and apparently the other cattle, signified the initials of the siblings' first names. If Melody recognized it, the smart deputy who was Casey undoubtedly did, too.

She would love to see these people arrested and prosecuted for what they'd done. And hopefully Casey and she would be there to testify against them in court.

But right now she was scared that they wouldn't remain alive that long.

She managed a glance at Casey. He was scowling, but when their eyes caught she saw something in them that she appreciated. No, despite their nights together, particularly the last one, they had no romantic relationship—although at the moment Melody kind of regretted that. She could die before this was all over, and it might be somehow easier if she died with the belief that someone as kind and determined as Deputy Colton had tried to save her, not just because it was his job, but because he *cared.*

She realized she felt the same about him, no matter what. And if they survived, was there a chance at a romantic relationship?

No matter how much she doubted it—still doubted she was ready for one—she hoped she had an opportunity to find out.

Chapter 20

Casey watched as Georgia and Delilah mounted their horses and walked them over the tamped-down grass toward where the nearest cows stood. The cattle stomped and mooed, as if they knew that something was about to happen.

Their lowing wasn't the only sound, though. Occasional planes flew overhead, but, more important, Casey heard vehicles in the distance moving along the road where they'd soon head.

Was that the way their backup would arrive? Assuming there was any, of course. It was a major assumption.

He looked over at Sean, who stayed on the ground with his gun aimed at Melody. Glancing down at his watch, Sean said, "I think it's near enough to the time the trucks are expected for us to get these cattle closer to the road to wait."

"Okay," Melody said. She glanced at Casey, and he read in her expression that she wanted to talk to him. Alone. Which wasn't going to happen.

But what *was* going to happen?

Was backup going to arrive? He'd definitely gotten the impression that was what Melody wanted to talk to him about, so he couldn't count on it.

He had an unpleasant feeling that Sean was about to shoot him. That way, they wouldn't have to worry about him while they moved the cattle and loaded them into whatever trucks were coming. Of course, he would remain alert and keep his gun in his hand, and use it if he needed to protect himself, though he wasn't sure how effective it would be under these circumstances. Would he be fast enough to raise his gun and shoot Sean before Sean shot him?

He was surprised, then, when Sean said, "You come along, too, Mr. Deputy. You can stay with Ms. Ranch Hand and me. I can see from the way you two look at each other that you've got something going, so I'll use both of you to keep the other under control. Just know that I won't kill either of you unless I need to so I can get the other one to do what I say. First shot probably won't be fatal then…probably. Got it?"

Yeah, he got it. And Casey wondered a bit about Sean's observation. Something going between Melody and him?

They apparently gave the impression they were

closer than they were. And that might not help them resolve this situation.

Well, if he ever was to get interested in another real relationship, she'd be at the top of his list of women to check out. Assuming, of course, that she had any interest, after her nasty divorce.

"Got it," he acknowledged aloud, and surprised himself by aiming a wink at Melody where she stood near the cattle as if priming herself to help out with herding them where their captors wanted. She sent back a weak, troubled smile, and he wished he could do something to reassure her. Of course, any reassurance right now could be a lie.

"First, though—hand over your gun now, Casey. I've let you hang on to it as a game, kind of. But I won't be able to watch you as closely now, so give it to me and I won't shoot your lady right now." Sean swung his arm up and took a few steps forward until the muzzle of his gun touched Melody's forehead. "Oh, and your phone, too. And yours, Melody."

Damn. But what choice did he have? Drawing closer to Sean, Casey considered whether he could shoot Sean now and end this, but Sean's finger was wiggling on the trigger as if to taunt him.

Plus, Delilah and Georgia had ridden closer, around the cows, and were watching.

Casey gave him his gun, grip first, and also pulled Melody's phone from his pocket and handed it to Sean, as Melody, too, gave him his phone. What choice did they have?

"Ha, ha!" Sean chortled. "Guess you're finally realizing who's in charge here." He kept his gun aimed again at Melody as he stuffed Casey's gun and both phones into his saddlebag. "And though I'm not sure what I'll do with you yet when the trucks arrive, at least this way you won't be able to call for help if I leave you here." He gestured with his weapon to wave Casey forward. "Let's go," he said. "And in case you need any other motivation to listen to me, Deputy, I'll be nice to both of you for now, until and unless there's a problem. You've already decided I'm a murderer—"

"Aren't you?" Casey asked wryly, unable to help himself from interrupting.

"Maybe, maybe not. But I could easily become one for the first, or not-so-first, time if I get any trouble from either of you. So keep that in mind, will you?" His gaze landed again on Melody, who remained still, and it morphed from somewhat amused to threatening. Casey had an urge to use the opportunity of having Sean's attention at least somewhat diverted to grab him and pull him down, but since he again trained his gun on Melody, that wasn't an option.

"Oh, I'll definitely keep it in mind," Melody said. She rolled her eyes as if she found the man who was menacing her merely stupid, not dangerous, too.

At least Sean didn't react to that. "Excellent. And Casey, how about you?"

"Oh, you can believe it's on my mind." And the look Casey leveled at Sean should tell him that he'd never forget it, never let it go.

Sean walked over to his horse, which he mounted, then aimed his gun again at Melody. "Okay," he said.

"We're going to get the cattle to the road. We've done well herding them while we're on horseback, but I know it can be done on foot, too, so that's what you'll do. Let's just all head toward the road and coax the cattle that way, too." He picked up a prod from his saddle with his left hand and waved it. "Haven't needed these much. You've trained those cattle well, Melody, from what I've seen. They start forward when we do, with one of us behind to wrangle the stragglers."

"That should work," Melody acknowledged.

"And do you have better ways? Bet you do," Sean called to her as he moved a bit away.

"Let's see how this goes" was all Melody said.

Then, with Georgia and Delilah once more on opposite sides of the herd and Sean behind with Melody near him, the cattle moved forward. Sean lagged a bit until Casey got closer to Melody.

"Hey, you can follow your lady," Sean said. "Help her out here, okay, Deputy?"

Casey wasn't sure what he should do, but for now all he did was stay a bit behind Melody but in front of Sean and his horse. The cattle kept moving, which was a good thing.

They went over a small rise, and that was when Casey saw the road ahead of them. There was a fence with a gate along it, so he figured this was part of Over-Herd Ranch, and Clarence Edison had built it out here to protect his cattle from getting onto the two-lane highway.

There was also a wide shoulder along each side of the road, outside the fence—wide enough that trucks could probably park on one side or the other while the cattle were being loaded. Casey figured the cattle would stop on this side of the fence, the gate would be opened, and people would get the cows onboard the trucks one at a time.

Melody could help with that, but he figured she'd hate it. Still, that might be a good time for her to talk to the drivers, if they didn't seem to realize what was happening. Or even if they did but hadn't realized human lives would be at stake.

And him? He'd just have to watch what was going on, wait…and hopefully find an opportunity to get Melody and himself out of this.

The cattle stopped near the fence, as Sean and his group likely wanted them to.

"Okay," Melody said, looking from Sean to Georgia and back. Delilah remained on horseback at the far side of the cattle herd. "You'll soon get these cows heading to wherever it is you're intending to sell them." She stopped for a moment and aimed a quizzical gaze toward Georgia, as if she assumed Sean's sister was the most likely to reveal that information, but Georgia just shrugged.

"You got it," Sean said. "And then we'll be out of here, too."

"You're getting into the trucks with them?" Casey asked.

"Could be," Sean replied.

"Are you also taking the horses?" Melody asked.

Casey figured she hoped they wouldn't so the two of them would have transportation back to the ranch house, assuming they were both allowed to stay there. And what good would it do to take Melody and him along, anyway? They'd just give the Dodds a hard time…as long as they weren't shot first. But Sean probably wouldn't leave horses with them. They'd get back to civilization and send the authorities after the trucks quicker.

If left here without their phones to call for help, they couldn't summon anyone else to go after the trucks. Still, they also would still be alive—or at least Casey hoped that was how Sean was currently thinking.

"We'll see." Sean gestured to Georgia, and the two of them moved a small distance away on their horses and began talking. Casey wasn't surprised that Sean still pointed his gun at Melody and him.

Casey used that as an opportunity, though, to get closer to Melody. "You okay?" he asked. She was pale, but her chin was raised resolutely as if she'd been through this kind of danger before and had come out just fine.

Which he doubted. But he still appreciated her bravery.

"I'll be better when they're gone," she said.

"Yeah, we both will. And even if they leave us here without horses—" He shut up for a few seconds as an SUV drove by, causing some of the leaves on the road shoulder to blow around. "We'll still be here, by the road, and we should be able to flag someone down for help."

"I hope so." She sounded so glum that he figured she believed Sean would shoot them before he left.

And Casey was worried about that, too.

For now, he looked her straight in the eyes, then moved close enough that he could have drawn her near and hugged her for emotional support—and more—if they weren't so visible to their enemies, who might find a way to use it against them.

Sean had, after all, seen some closeness between them that Casey had been trying not to acknowledge to himself…much.

But now—well, once this was over and they returned to whatever reality they could, maybe he really would see where the familiarity they'd begun could lead them.

For the moment, Casey attempted to put all thoughts of Melody and how they'd get along in the future to the back of his mind.

He needed to watch, wait and figure out what to do to save them now.

There they were—or at least Melody assumed the two semis rolling slowly toward them along the road were the vehicles Sean and his co-conspirators were waiting for. When the trucks began to slow down, she felt even more sure.

"Woo-hoo!" called out Sean from behind her, the ultimate confirmation about whether those were the ones he had hired.

The five of them—the Dodds, Casey and Melody—now stood along the fence with the cattle just behind them. They watched as the trucks came to a stop and parked on the shoulder.

So how would things work out now? Melody knew Sean wanted to have her help get the cattle inside the trailers. Would he also insist that she go along with them in the trucks to wherever he planned to sell the cows?

Sell them. The stolen cows that were her responsibility were about to be finally taken away for good, and she would be part of that, like it or not. They wouldn't even necessarily be identifiable as OverHerd Ranch cattle unless people studied them closely. Presumably the brands on all of them had been changed as Addie, the dead cow's, had been—from OHR to SG.

Where would Casey be when she left with the Dodds? Melody wondered. Would he ride along with them? Stay here, alive and well?

She didn't even want to consider the alternative.

She forced herself to concentrate when two men got out of the cab of the first truck. She assumed the occupants of the other truck's cab would join them, though she couldn't see them yet.

"Gentlemen!" Sean called. "Thanks for coming. Now, show us how we should load the cattle, and we'll begin, okay?"

The two men had reached the gate, where Sean met them. Melody noted that Georgia now held a gun and was trying to be surreptitious about it as she kept it trained on Casey. Was it the same gun that Sean had held? Melody didn't think so—and that made her swallow in sadness.

It might have been Pierce's that they'd taken from him when they killed him.

In any case, it was a symbol that Casey and she had better not tell these other people what was really going on here.

And so she wouldn't—for now, at least.

"That sounds good," said the taller of the two men, who was clean-shaven and wore a gray cap with a logo Melody couldn't see and a dark blue sweatshirt with matching trousers. He'd come from the driver's side of the truck. The other man, shorter and with a receding hairline, was dressed similarly but wore no cap.

Presumably, they knew they'd be transporting cattle in their truck. Was that why there were two of them?

"We'll bring the first cow through the gate as an example, to see how this works out," Delilah said loudly enough for all of them to hear, which Melody found almost amusing since she doubted the accountant would do anything but watch the cows get into the truck.

And what about how they would smell in the trucks? Out in the pasture, their aromas weren't particularly bad in the open air, but inside?

Well, these truckers had apparently been told what they were getting into. Maybe they'd even transported cattle before.

Melody glanced at Casey, who was at her side. He had a bland expression on his face. For now, at least. Would he attempt to tell the truck guys what was going on? Probably, if he had the opportunity, and she would do the same.

He probably wouldn't want to start any trouble now, though, like revealing what the situation was. These drivers were potentially in as much trouble as Casey and she were. If they gave any of the Dodds a hard time, one or more of them might get shot. Casey would undoubtedly try to protect them, too.

Before any of the cows were wrangled through the gate, two more people joined them from the other truck, a woman and a man. They wore similar outfits. Maybe that was standard for this transportation company. The vehicles themselves all had the same logo on them, a loopy, floral thing that Melody wasn't familiar with.

"Hi," the woman called. "Are we ready to get the cattle loaded on board?"

Everyone but Casey and Melody seemed to say yes. Over the next few minutes, one cow was culled from the front of the herd and led through the fence by Georgia, with Melody assisting, per Sean's instructions. There was a ramp at the back of the trailer that the cow was able to walk up, with the people leading her.

The inside of the trailer looked clean enough, Melody thought. She had no idea how many of the cows would fit in here, but since there were only eleven, and two trucks, having six in this one should be okay.

Another cow was led inside by Sean and his wife. Delilah appeared to be fine with helping out here, even if she wasn't as much of a ranch-type person as the others.

Casey accompanied them, and Melody assumed that was because of Sean's insistence…and additional threats, since he seemed inclined to have Casey accompany Delilah and him to the front of the trailer.

As a result, the five of them who'd headed here via the pasture were now inside the truck, along with all four of the drivers, temporarily for now, Melody figured, to get things started.

Only two cows were in there so far, so which people

would return outside and lead the next one in? Melody just stood there, waiting to see if she, the ranch hand, was designated to help with that.

And where were Sean and Georgia's guns now? She didn't see them being pointed at anyone, not even surreptitiously. Did that mean there would be an opportunity to run once they returned outside?

She figured, though, from Sean's prior threats, that Casey and she would be given their instructions and remain separated, rather than being given the chance to flee together right now. The threat would remain that if one was able to get away, the other would get shot in retribution.

What were they going to do?

Casey wished he could plan something to save them—and not just Melody and him. It had become his responsibility to try to rescue the other innocent civilians who were now involved—the truck drivers.

Although there was something about them that made him wonder how innocent they were. All four of them acted like the drivers they were as they stood with Melody and him. But he'd noted that those drivers seemed to be studying the five of them, as they discussed their instructions, when the other cattle would be brought inside, and the route they would take to get to the ranch in northern Arizona where the Dodds apparently intended to sell the cows. Had they heard of the theft? Did they know what was going on?

Were they okay with driving a bunch of stolen cattle this way? He wondered how much Sean had offered to pay them.

Maybe they were watching him for some indication of whether they could demand more—from the person who'd stolen these valuable cows.

But there was something about them that suggested there was more to this part of the situation than Casey had figured out.

He'd just have to wait and see.

Suddenly, someone ran up the ramp and into the back of the trailer.

Someone pointing a gun toward Sean.

At the same time, all four drivers also pulled weapons from their pockets and aimed at Georgia and Delilah.

And Casey erupted into laughter, nodding happily as Melody aimed a confused gaze toward him.

The man who'd run up the ramp didn't meet Casey's gaze, though, and he knew full well why he didn't. Instead, the guy used his free hand to pull something out of his pocket—his identification.

"FBI," he said. "Sean Dodd, Georgia Dodd and Delilah Kennedy Dodd, you are under arrest for the murder of Pierce Tostig, an act of violent crime."

"What!" Sean shouted, and he started digging into his own pocket, presumably for his gun. But the female driver grabbed his hands and wrestled them behind his back, where she cuffed him and pulled out his gun, sticking it into her own waistband.

The other FBI agents frisked Georgia and Delilah

and apparently found only the one additional gun. Soon they, too, were cuffed.

And as the Dodds were all led down the ramp, one by one, sirens sounded in the distance. Clearly, official help was on the way, so no one would have to drive these criminals to town in the semitrucks.

That gave Casey time to do as he'd wanted to for the last few minutes. He hurried to Melody's side.

"FBI?" She sounded confused. "Why are they here? I wouldn't have thought this was their jurisdiction."

"Probably not, normally," Casey agreed. But he looked toward the agent who'd run up the ramp and begun the arrest process. "Hey," he said, giving the agent a high five. And then he turned back toward Melody. "Melody Hayworth, I'd like you to meet my twin brother, Everett. My older brother, Agent Everett Colton." He turned back to Everett, whose grin was enormous. "So what brought you here, bro?" Casey asked.

Chapter 21

Melody remained standing next to Casey on the road-side near the trucks. She felt relieved. Was this over at last? It appeared that way. And how interesting that Casey's brother Everett, from the FBI, had been the agent in charge of bringing this to an end. The official Sur County Sheriff's Department black SUVs had already picked up the real truck drivers a mile down the road and they were being interrogated about what they knew about the cattle rustling, if anything.

Melody gathered from the shouted discussion that the FBI agents had commandeered the semis so they could dash out here undercover to apprehend the rogue cattle rustlers—the Dodds. And even if they were cleared quickly of any wrongdoing those real drivers wouldn't be able to take off with their trucks, not with the cows still inside.

Fortunately, the agents had found Melody's phone, along with Casey's, in the saddlebag still on Sean's horse, located with the other Dodd mounts behind the fence near the road. Though the phones would be evidence in the multiple crimes the Dodds had committed, Everett handed them to Casey and her, anyway—a good thing. She really needed hers.

She called Clarence. The ranch owner was thrilled to hear that the cows were now safely in Melody's control, and the rustlers had been apprehended. "By Everett Colton, I presume."

"Yes, and some other FBI agents," Melody responded, keeping her curiosity about what Clarence knew to herself. Getting the cattle back to the main ranch land was paramount.

And, of course, that was Clarence's opinion, too. He promised to send a few other ranch hands there via the road—and Melody promised she'd make sure the five horses, including Casey's and hers, were available for them to help herd the cows back where they belonged. Surely, with the Dodds no longer in charge, that would be the case.

"And you?" Clarence asked. "I assume you'd rather just come back here, right? That's what I want. I need to hear your story about what happened and how it got resolved."

"Fine." Melody felt a bit relieved that she wouldn't be one of the drovers on the way back. She needed some time off.

And…well, she didn't need to remain with Casey right now, but she wanted to. If nothing else, she wanted to learn how he had secretly worked with Everett so that this situation came to a positive conclusion.

But she also hoped to stay in Casey's company just a little longer. No, they didn't really have a relationship, despite their wonderful one-night stand. But she hoped they would see each other occasionally, as friends who had successfully worked together and helped to resolve a difficult situation.

But despite all they had been through together, she still wasn't ready for anything beyond that. Wasn't sure she'd ever be.

Although if she ever was, Casey would definitely be her pick…

And he seemed to value the idea of her being a ranch hand.

In any case, when she ended her conversation with Clarence, she invited both Casey and Everett to join her at the ranch house to provide a summary to the town selectman about what had happened.

"I'm going to check with my fellow deputies about the status of things around here," said Casey from beside her. "Hopefully, we'll all head back to town soon."

"Let's go get our horses before anything else," Melody told him, and they did. Fortunately, both Witchy and Cal were where they'd tethered them and seemed happy enough to be walked to the nearby roadside. The activity around the official sheriff's department vehicles had quieted down, and Melody was happy to join Casey there after they tied up their horses inside the pasture fence near where the Dodds' steeds had been secured.

Casey was soon met by Jeremy Krester. "Glad you're okay," the sheriff said. "Both of you." But the tall, thin man with graying hair leveled his gaze mostly at Casey, his deputy.

"I see you have a bunch of our guys here, too—including Captain Walter Forman and Deputy Bob Andrews." Casey glanced toward Melody. She recalled meeting both of them when the helicopter had arrived to pick up poor Pierce.

She asked, "Is the other emergency over?"

Casey stared at her. "Other emergency?"

The sheriff appeared a bit embarrassed. "Yeah, though we haven't yet caught the perpetrators. Like I said, it was an armed robbery, but by the time we got there, it was over and the perps had disappeared. No indication yet where they are. I probably should just have sent more of our deputies out here to help you."

"Well, we're okay now," Casey said. "Interesting, though, that the FBI helped out this way."

Melody had the sense he was rubbing his boss's nose into his possible mistake, but she didn't say anything.

Still, having a federal agency like the FBI here, represented by a deputy's brother, resolving things did sound a bit off to her—something she might see on TV or a movie.

Everett stood on the road shoulder near the three official vehicles that still had their red lights flashing on top. Melody wished she could bombard him with questions, but this wasn't the time…or, most likely, the place.

But right now, she couldn't have been happier to meet Casey's older brother—who was also in law enforcement and apparently had been instrumental in getting out here to bring down the Dodds and save the cattle.

"Good job," Everett called to Deputy Andrews, who was about to get into the driver's seat of the second SUV. There was a third one, too, behind it.

Melody couldn't help it. She peered inside that second SUV. Sean and Delilah were ensconced in the middle seat, with deputies both in front of them and behind them.

They remained in cuffs, from what Melody could see. And though they'd shot dirty looks at both Casey and her from the moment they were taken into custody, she doubted they'd have an opportunity to exact any revenge.

Speaking of teasing, she had an urge to yell something inside to them, taunt them about their failure, the fact the cattle would go back to their normal lives, but these thieves—and murderers—certainly wouldn't.

But why bother? It wouldn't really make her feel any better. Besides, judging by their posture and expressions, they already knew their despicable escapade was over, and so was their freedom to try to harm anyone else this way, or any other way, including cattle.

Melody considered peeking inside the first of the police vehicles where Georgia was detained, but decided not to. She figured she'd see all of them again eventually.

In fact, she'd look forward to testifying at trial against them.

Everett began talking then, and when she turned back toward him, she noticed he was on the phone. In a minute, his call was over, and he faced Casey, who now stood close to Melody.

"Hey, bro," he said. "We've been officially summoned to the ranch house—you, me and Melody—to provide our esteemed selectman and ranch owner a rundown of all that happened."

Which Melody was already aware of, but Clarence's invitation definitely made it official.

It would be interesting to hear their takes as they described all they knew, all that had happened, to Clarence, along with her.

Casey was fine with the idea of talking with Selectman Edison again, especially since Melody would be along. Not to mention his hero brother, Everett.

He wasn't surprised, though, that they had to wait until the first two of the three department vehicles, the ones containing the prisoners, took off for the station. Clarence Edison was sending some of his remaining ranch hands to take charge of wrangling the cattle back to their more usual environment in the closer pastures.

Fortunately, though, Clarence was more interested in having Melody join them for their discussion than having her do any herding right now. She'd remain in Casey's presence a while longer, which was fine with him.

He'd talked briefly with Everett and Sheriff Krester. Yes, the FBI team, with Everett in charge, had been the ones to initially place the Dodds under arrest, but that was for convenience, since they'd gotten to this area first, although Casey realized there was more to the delay than that.

However, the local authorities were taking over. The legal proceedings—arraignments, trials and all—would occur in this area, where the evidence and witnesses were.

There were reasons, though, why Everett and his FBI contingent had happened to be present in Cactus Creek, and the brief mentions in the conversation suggested that Selectman Edison had had something to do with that.

Which made Casey even more eager for this upcoming meeting.

Especially since, fortunately, his initial suspect, Clarence's ex-wife Hilda, apparently hadn't been involved in the rustling, which would have made this conversation difficult.

"Hey, there they are!" Melody, standing near the remaining department vehicle beside him, pointed toward another SUV that was approaching from down the road. The white vehicle sported the OverHerd Ranch name and logo, with the head of a cow on its side.

Four men and two women got out and greeted Melody effusively once she'd approached them, giving her hugs and exclaiming that they hoped she was all right.

Casey felt irritated when the men hugged her, then he castigated himself. Melody and he were just friends. Colleagues who'd gone through a lot.

Two people who'd attempted to ease a difficult situation by having a night of passionate sex…

Which he'd need to forget, or at least not keep thinking about. It was done, it had been a good thing, and now it was over.

Although…well, the fact that Melody seemed even more beautiful now, while she was happy and relieved and surrounded by friends dressed like her in work clothes for a cattle drive, somehow made it harder for him to simply stick the memory of their wonderful night at the back of his mind.

But he would.

In a short while, Melody had helped her fellow ranch hands get the cattle back out of the trucks and secured behind the fence of the ranch land, though one of the men drove the SUV they'd arrived in back to the ranch house.

That gave the semi drivers, who'd been milling around, the go-ahead to take back possession of their vehicles and get on the road, but not before they had been interviewed and gave their contact information to Captain Forman. Evidently they did not appear to have known what the Dodds were up to.

And after that, it was finally time for Casey and the rest to get on the road, too—a good thing, since daylight was beginning to fade, and there certainly weren't any streetlights out here on this remote road.

Casey took charge of the remaining sheriff's department vehicle, promising to drop off Walter at the station before he, Melody and Everett, also riding with him, returned to the ranch to talk to Selectman Clarence.

This had been quite an interesting, revealing day… and Casey recognized it wasn't over yet.

Melody was back at the ranch house. Not exactly her home, the apartment in one of the auxiliary bunkhouses near here, but Clarence's house.

This time, she was there with both Casey and his brother. They'd complied with the summons by her boss, and they had a story to tell.

Melody hoped she learned something, too.

As he had the last time, before Casey and she had gone on their adventure to bring back the stolen cattle, Clarence had them shown through the wooden entryway into his ornate living room to talk. He soon joined them, having a member of the help, whom Melody had seen before but not met, bring them coffee, promising drinks later since he intended that they all stay for dinner.

Clarence took over one of the sections of the room's brown leather sofas. He gestured for Melody and the two Colton brothers to take seats on other portions of the sofa facing him.

Then it was time to talk.

"Hey, you three," Clarence said in his usually jovial tone—the one he used when he wasn't upset about stolen cattle. He started to joke about how lonesome he'd been without some of his cattle and one of his favorite ranch hands—he looked at Melody, which made her smile, despite knowing he was kidding—plus his favorite sheriff's deputy and FBI agent abandoning him for a while.

A good, useful while, he admitted.

Looking at Everett, Casey spoke first. "You know I'm always glad to see you, bro, but why did you happen to be around here to save me?"

"Oh, you can thank our favorite selectman." He turned toward Clarence, whose senior face lit up in a huge smile. "He happened to call my superiors in Phoenix and expressly request that I be sent here with a team of agents because he said some federal laws were being broken and he needed help."

"Help my department wasn't providing just then," Casey said, shaking his head.

"Exactly," Clarence responded. He told the story from his perspective, probably exaggerating a bit.

Melody gathered from what Clarence said that he'd been irritated when Pierce happened to disappear right when she, who was less experienced, headed out with Deputy Sheriff Casey to find the missing cattle. Pierce's job had been to help oversee care of the remaining cattle.

"I wanted him back," Clarence said. "I also considered calling the sheriff about this but figured he already had someone in the field from that office chasing his cattle—Casey. So I called a superior in the Phoenix FBI office and asked him to send our buddy Everett Colton, who knows the Cactus Creek area well, to try to find a missing ranch hand. And, of course, it didn't hurt that Casey is Everett's brother."

Clarence had claimed there was the possibility of a violent crime being committed—one of the areas where the FBI had jurisdiction—although he hadn't yet known of Pierce's death. As a result, with Casey still out in the field, Everett and his team members had been sent.

And Clarence had demanded silence—that Everett not attempt to contact his brother, at least not yet.

By the time they arrived, Pierce's body and the dead cow had been found, making the situation clearly a violent crime. Pierce's horse had shown up soon afterward near the stable. Everett and his colleagues stayed in town to work with the sheriff—and the selectman—in sorting out any evidence. That was why they were there to investigate after Melody called the sheriff's department on Casey's phone for help.

"And it worked," Clarence affirmed as the conversation drew to a close. "Don't get me wrong, I'm generally happy with the job our local sheriff's department does." He leveled a grin at Casey, who nodded back.

Melody noted the word *generally*, but didn't comment. She figured Casey had focused on it, too, since he quickly shared a glance with Everett.

"But, hey, you. Agent Everett Colton." This time Clarence focused directly on Everett. "You're F-B-I like you guys!"

Melody shook her head slightly in amusement. Her boss was clearly back to being himself, now that this nasty interlude was drawing to a close.

He was once again a punster.

He soon shepherded them all into his dining room, where they shared a delicious dinner—most likely the only one of theirs Clarence would pay for, despite the discussion Melody and Casey had had previously. Casey and she had shared their tale of life in the pasture chasing the missing cattle. Not all details about it, though, such as how their nights were spent—especially the last one.

Clarence let them know that he'd sent a couple of ranch hands out to retrieve Addie's remains and bury them behind the barn. That sounded appropriate to Melody.

When dinner was over, Clarence again thanked them all and then ushered them from his ranch house and out of his company.

"Would you like a ride to town?" Everett asked Casey as Melody stood with them on the front porch, which was fortunately well-lit at this late hour.

"No, thanks. My car's already here. I left it the other day when we headed off to find the cattle."

"Great job with that." Everett smiled at Casey, then gave him a brotherly hug. "I'll probably see you in town, at least over the next few days. I'm hanging around till we're sure the case against your Dodd buddies is getting well-established."

"Great about your staying for a while," Casey said. "And those felons are far from buddies of mine, but I assume Sean and you aren't friends any longer."

"You assume right, of course. Anyway, nice meeting you, Melody." He gave her a hearty handshake, then looked from her face to Casey's, as if searching for something.

Melody sighed inside but didn't say anything. He obviously wasn't about to find anything between them. Which in a way was a shame…although it was for the best.

Still…

Melody at least derived some happiness from the fact

that Casey walked her back to the bunkhouse containing her apartment, though he didn't go inside.

Just in case… "Would you like to come in for a drink?" she asked. "A quick one, of course." She said the latter in case he considered that an invitation for more.

"Not tonight, thanks." Casey dashed her hopes of most likely seeing much of him, if at all, even though he'd limited his refusal to that night. But if there was to be anything more to their friendship, wouldn't he just come in for a minute?

"That's fine," she said cheerfully, anyway.

"Let's grab a drink or a dinner in town someplace soon," Casey said. "No hassle that way, and I'd like to stay in touch. Okay?"

"Fine," Melody said, realizing that this was Casey's nice effort to make sure they went their separate ways.

It certainly was better that way. She hadn't changed her mind about not wanting a real relationship…had she?

Well, if so, it obviously wouldn't be with Casey, no matter how sexy she found him.

And so, under the light by the front door to her building, she stood on tiptoe, reached up and pulled Casey's mouth down to hers for a kiss. A brief one.

It shouldn't feel so hot, she thought.

Well, so what? She moved away and managed to send him a smile. "Good night," she said. "And thanks for all you did to save those cattle."

Then she hurriedly opened the door and dashed inside.

Chapter 22

Casey, sitting in his crowded, shared office at the sheriff's department, should have continued to feel delighted several days after his return with Melody.

The Dodds were in custody. Plus he'd had some additional success yesterday, after his return. Along with a couple of other deputies, including Bob Andrews, he had located and arrested the suspects in the clothing-store robbery. A very satisfying conclusion to that situation, too—assuming the criminals were found guilty of armed robbery at trial.

Fortunately, they hadn't hurt anyone during the robbery. And considering the evidence from the robbery that he and Bob had found at the apartment shared by the suspects, a pair of students who were attending college at a Tucson university, that should be a slam dunk.

Casey was, in fact, delighted about that achievement. What he hadn't been delighted about, at first, was his urge to call Melody and tell her about it.

He hadn't seen her since their dinner at the ranch owner's home. That was probably a good thing. And why would he? He had no reason to go to her ranch, and if she'd had any reason to come to town she hadn't told him about it.

Which was fine.

He could have let her know that he had finished providing all the information and evidence that he could against the Dodds right away. From his perspective, the case was closed—and there shouldn't be even a shred of possibility that those killers and rustlers wouldn't be found guilty and put away for the rest of their pathetic lives.

But right now, he was furious.

"Why?" he demanded angrily of Sheriff Krester, who'd just told him the Dodds were out on bail. "You know what they're like. They'll just run."

"And then you'll just have to catch them again," the sheriff said, eyeing Casey with a half-amused, half-irritated lifting of his gray eyebrows. "I'm sure you'll do it just fine."

"Yeah, right. Like last time. But—"

"No, you're right. You shouldn't be put in that position. *We* shouldn't be put in that position. But the Dodds apparently hired some pretty good lawyers—some new criminal attorneys who just opened an office here, I gather. I didn't know them, though I was there in court. The Dodds had their arraignment earlier today and, yeah, they were allowed out on bail, even though the charges include first-degree murder, and bail in that situation might not be legal. How'd they do it? Bribe the judge? Who knows?"

Jeremy came farther inside and sat down on a chair facing Casey's desk. Casey leaned forward on his elbows and clenched his fists. Not that he'd strike his boss, or anyone. It was his fury causing him to react.

Bob was there, too, along with their other officemate, Deputy David Young. Both of them also looked at their boss with expressions that were almost accusatory. But Casey knew full well that the sheriff's department did not have a final say whether or not the judge allowed bail. All they could do was testify at the eventual trial, provide evidence...and hope justice would prevail.

"The thing is," the sheriff said, "it came out at the arraignment that Sean and Delilah have a six-month-old daughter. They'd had a neighbor who also did babysitting for them watching little Kennedy, and they'd apparently planned all along to drop Delilah off in town with her while Sean and Georgia dealt with the cattle."

"Another indication those Dodds are all lowlifes. Poor kid." And it was another reason Casey was glad he hadn't wound up marrying Georgia. But he hadn't imagined any of them would get involved with murder and rustling, let alone insufficient care of a child.

"Yeah," the sheriff agreed.

Something else occurred to Casey. "Well, even if they were granted bail, how could they afford it?" he demanded. "Or even the payment to a bail bondsman?

They stole those cattle because they needed money, or at least that's what they told me."

"Obviously we don't have all the answers," Jeremy said. He shrugged and left the office.

Well, the only good thing about that was that it gave Casey a reason to call Melody. She needed to know about the Dodds' release. And the baby? Maybe.

But would they go after Melody, or him, in retribution? If they were smart, the Dodds would simply behave like good citizens and not call attention to themselves, at least not until after their trial. Hopefully then, they'd be in prison for a good long time and not out in the world and able to murder people—or steal cattle. And hopefully they had a relative or two Casey didn't know about who could take care of the baby.

But there was no reason to believe they were particularly smart.

Casey glanced at his computer. It was nearly three o'clock in the afternoon. Not the best time to call a ranch hand, he was sure. But the sooner, the better. Worst case, he could leave a message.

He walked out of his office, leaving Bob behind. He doubted that anything he'd say would be private, but just in case...

First, though, before calling Melody, he found a corner at the end of the hallway. Then he phoned his brother. Everett would be interested in this, too. He and his fellow FBI team members had been the ones who'd first captured the Dodds, after all. He had even hung around for the next couple of days, also helping to put together evidence, though he'd gone back to Phoenix yesterday. While in Cactus Creek, he had also visited Casey, who lived in a small house at the rear of their parents' sizable property.

Casey was quite happy living there. He could spend time with their folks, yet have privacy, too. But he and Everett had visited for an evening's dinner. And he'd soon enjoy Thanksgiving with them, too. Plus there was their upcoming Christmas dinner, an annual event they all enjoyed, and Everett would most likely be around for it, as well, though he wasn't coming back for Thanksgiving, which was usually a much smaller affair and seldom included guests, let alone all family members.

He still believed that Melody would join them for Christmas, after his earlier invitation to her. He hoped so, at least.

"Hey, Everett," he said when his brother answered the phone. "How are things in Phoenix?"

"Fine, but why are you really calling now?" Everett asked.

Casey already knew his brother was smart. He gave a rundown of what the sheriff had told him.

"Damn," Everett growled. "And there's a baby involved, too? What a mess."

Casey promised to stay in touch and keep Everett informed about anything new he heard.

When they hung up, it was time to call Melody. He was eager to hear her voice, even though that was so unwise. But he missed her companionship more than he'd ever thought possible.

He thought about inviting her to town to join him

for coffee and he would reveal what had been going on, but he was on duty and it was better to tell her fast.

"Good to hear from you, Casey," she said after answering the phone. "I can't talk long, though. I'm out in the pasture with part of our herd—and that includes the wonderful cows we rescued. They're doing fine."

"Glad to hear that. And the reason I'm calling is to make sure you stay alert." He revealed the information about the Dodds now being out on bail. And because he knew this woman who cared so much about cattle would undoubtedly also care about one of the reasons they probably got out so fast, pending their preliminary hearing, he also revealed the fact that they had a child. But he additionally told her about how they'd abandoned that baby.

"What horrible people!" Melody exclaimed.

Casey could do nothing but agree.

And when they hung up only a minute later, he had another urge to see Melody again.

Bad idea, he reminded himself, and headed back to his office.

Melody was shocked, even as she stared around the part of the pasture where she now rode on Cal's back and wrangled the cattle with some of her fellow ranch hands.

She'd known the Dodds were terrible, but how could they have left their daughter that way? Bad enough they were cattle rustlers, not to mention murderers.

She appreciated Casey's call for the warning it contained. She'd certainly try to stay even more alert, but she recognized that, after all that had happened, she had become watchful and concerned and extremely vigilant, even while doubting anyone would dare to try to rustle any more cattle around here.

And…well, she hated to admit it to herself, but she did miss Casey, his strong and sexy presence while they'd been in the fields together, and, even more, his kindness. And even his sense of humor when he'd kidded her at times about what a ranch hand did.

In fact, after they hung up, she impulsively called him back. "You know, Thanksgiving's next week," she said. "I'm helping to cook a great dinner for the other ranch hands who live in my bunkhouse and would love to have you join us."

"Sorry," he responded immediately, and the word made her heart sink. "But I'll be joining my parents, as usual."

He didn't mention his prior invitation for her to join his family at Christmas and she didn't ask.

It probably wasn't going to happen.

She'd probably see Casey again sometime, in town or wherever.

But she was just going to have to get over him.

Thanksgiving. Damn, how Casey had appreciated Melody's invitation, he thought, returning to his office.

But it would have been a bad idea in many ways for him to accept. For one thing, his parents expected him.

For another…well, something that could seem even more than an ordinary date, which he didn't intend to follow up on with Melody, anyway, was out of the question. Or was it?

Sitting back down at his desk, he looked at his computer to learn what his next assignment was. He needed to go check on some alleged vandalism outside a local bank.

Good. That would keep him busy for a while.

As did other assignments over the next few days. That made it easier—somewhat—not to think about the Dodds a lot. Except to stay watchful.

And Melody? Well, thoughts of her seemed to creep into his mind, so he cast them aside and found other things to concentrate on. Or at least he tried.

And then, a few days later, Casey received a call demanding his presence at the Sur County courthouse, which wasn't far from the sheriff's department in Cactus Creek. Jeremy Krester was told to come, too.

"What's this about?" Casey asked as they strode down the street on the way to the courthouse.

"Don't know, but I gather it has something to do with the Dodds," Sheriff Krester responded, shaking his head in the cool November breeze so his gray hair wisped around his face.

Casey felt his own hair moving on his forehead, too. "Did they do something else? Did they disappear while out on bail so we're needed to find them again?"

"We'll find out," the sheriff said.

But the reason was quite different from that. The district attorney, Warren Marano, stood up before Judge Morley Ackerman, who was seated on the bench in the courtroom. The judge was fortysomething, stern and wore a standard black robe, with only a fringe of brown hair on his head.

And Marano? There was no mistaking the shock on Marano's face, as his jaw dropped.

What was going on?

It was soon time for Casey to feel shocked, too. Especially when Georgia walked into the courtroom and down the aisle carrying a baby.

Sean and Delilah's? If so, why? And where were *they*?

District Attorney Marano asked for their attention. There weren't many onlookers in the seats, and he seemed to talk directly to the sheriff, who sat beside Casey.

"We have a major development in the prosecution of Sean and Delilah Dodd," Marano began.

That didn't surprise Casey, considering the fact this session was being held and the sheriff had been asked to come.

"It seems that two of our suspects, Sean Dodd and his wife, Delilah Dodd, committed suicide."

Oh, no. Casey might have hated what they'd done, but he'd certainly never anticipated this. Shock pulsed through his veins.

"No!" That shriek came from Georgia, who was sitting in the front row. It caused the baby in her arms to start crying. "They'd never commit suicide," Georgia shouted. "Someone must have murdered them."

How had Georgia wound up with the baby? Had Sean and Delilah left the little girl in her care rather than the neighbor's, knowing they were about to kill themselves? Casey wished he knew the answers to that and more.

Ackerman had a clerk come over and escort Georgia, with the baby, from the courtroom, at least for now.

Then Marano continued, describing what had apparently happened. "Last night, they were driving on Sheldon Street, where the town's shopping mall is located. They apparently began speeding and rammed right into the parking lot wall. They both were killed—and there was a suicide note in the car, taped to the dashboard."

Well, there went at least part of the prosecution of those murderers and rustlers. Georgia was still around, though, and she was as much to blame in the whole thing as her brother and sister-in-law.

And what a horrible ending for those two. But according to the note the DA went on to describe, they would rather die than face prison.

Georgia was brought back into the courtroom, the baby still in her arms. She pleaded with the judge to absolve her of all charges so she could take care of her niece.

"You're still out on bail," Judge Ackerman reminded her. "Be sure to return for your preliminary hearing, and bring your attorney. We'll see how that argument goes."

Casey felt sorry for the baby but didn't think a sudden desire to take care of an orphaned family member would clear Georgia. And was that how Sean and Delilah would have wanted things? If they'd committed suicide, they'd probably left instructions for what they wanted for their daughter.

What Georgia had screamed stuck with him, though. When the sheriff and he left the courtroom a while later, Casey excused himself and called Everett to let him know what had happened. "Georgia yelled that Sean and Delilah would never commit suicide. She claimed they'd likely been murdered." He paused. "I'm sure I'm not going to be assigned to look into it, but what do you think?"

"I think I'm going to head in your direction again soon—maybe using a Thanksgiving vacation as an excuse—and look into it, just in case."

"That's my great big brother," Casey said before ending the call. "Look forward to seeing you again soon."

He walked back to the department with the sheriff, who, as Casey also assumed, just chalked up Georgia's cry about possible murder to her grief. "There was a suicide note," he reminded Casey.

Casey didn't bother to mention that could have been planted by the murderer. Had the couple been assaulted before being put into the car and aimed toward the wall?

And would they ever find out?

Well, Everett on the case might be quite helpful in determining the truth.

But more deaths. Sure, Casey might have detested Sean and Delilah for what they had done, but he hadn't wished them dead.

For the rest of the day, what was left of it, Casey couldn't concentrate. Sure, he saw a lot of nasty things as a deputy sheriff, but this somehow really got into him.

People died, however it occurred. Life wasn't a sure thing.

And his life? Oh, it was okay the way it was…yet all of this made him think of Melody again.

A lot.

As his workday ended, he called her, hoping she was back at the ranch. She sounded surprised to hear from him, yet somehow happy. At least she didn't hang up on him. And, yes, it was getting late enough that the cattle were all enclosed behind fencing for the night.

"Can I come see you now?" he said. "I'll come to your ranch, if that's okay."

"Sure," she said. "Sounds good. See you soon."

See her soon? *Yeah!*

As he hung up and closed down his computer so he could get out of there, he thought about seeing Melody. Now—and in the future?

That sounded so good.

Had he gotten over whatever his hang-ups were about starting a relationship?

Maybe.

He had a feeling he'd figure it out that night.

Casey was coming here? Melody was in a stall in the barn, brushing Cal and combing his long, soft mane after removing his saddle for the night.

Why? And why was she looking forward so much to seeing Casey?

Well, she knew the answer to that last question. She missed him. The bond they'd formed while following the cattle, chasing down the rustlers and spending nights together felt unbreakable.

Unless, of course, he was coming here to deliver some kind of blow, like he was moving away, or he'd found a girlfriend…whatever. She'd find out soon.

She finished with Cal and returned to her apartment, where she quickly showered and changed into a nice gray shirt and black slacks, better looking and better smelling than the outfit she had worn at work that day. She left her hair loose, not in its ponytail.

Then she exited the building and walked to the main ranch house, which was the first thing Casey would see as he entered the ranch property again.

She had to smile. It wasn't even Thanksgiving yet, but Clarence had already had at least the outside of his long, one-story red house decorated for Christmas. There were wreaths around the door, and lights mounted around the windows; they weren't lit yet despite the current darkness of twilight. A string of holly had also been attached at the sides of the couple of steps up to the porch.

And most amusing was that he had had mistletoe hung a couple of places from the top of the porch roof. Was Clarence planning on kissing visitors to his ranch?

For now, though, she glanced at her phone after pulling it from her pocket. It had been about half an hour since she'd talked with Casey, so he should arrive any-time now…she hoped. For now, she stood at the side of the porch, waiting.

Maybe, if he'd be here a while, they could go sit on the porch to talk. The mistletoe was spread out enough that they could just ignore it and not walk underneath it.

Although…well, the idea was tempting but unwise.

Sure enough, a car passed through the gate at the base of the driveway. Casey's dark SUV, which resembled, but wasn't, an official sheriff's vehicle, pulled up and parked near the porch.

Casey got out. He was still in his deputy uniform…

and looked good in it. And now that they were back in town, he was clean-shaven.

Melody smiled. Broadly. She was so glad to see him.

But she didn't know why he'd wanted to get together that evening. Maybe something was wrong. And so she just stood there, swallowing her smile, crossing her arms in front of her chest.

"Hi, Melody," he called, then joined her where she stood. She considered giving him a welcoming kiss but didn't.

She still didn't know why he'd come.

"Look, there are a few things I want to discuss with you. Can we just go sit up there?" He pointed toward the porch. "Although, if Clarence is home and he can hear us, that won't be a good idea."

"I don't believe he's home yet. Plus he had his house built to be perfect in every way, or so he says. In any case, it's supposed to be soundproof."

"Hope so." Casey reached out and took her hand, leading her onto the porch, where they sat facing one another on a couple of the fancy vinyl deck chairs there.

"So what's up?" Melody attempted to sound cheerful, but her concern rose. The expression on Casey's wonderfully handsome face was bland, and gave nothing away.

"Let me get the bad stuff out of the way first, okay?"

Bad stuff. Melody drew in her breath. "Sure," she said.

And it really was bad. She certainly didn't like Sean and Delilah Dodd, but she hadn't wished them dead. Imprisoned forever, yes.

The fact that they had a baby they'd left behind during the pasture trek only made things worse. What would happen to the child now? Casey said that Georgia had brought the six-month-old, a girl named Kennedy, to court and was apparently caring for her now, but Georgia still could—and hopefully would—go to prison for a good long time.

Casey had no answer for what would happen to the child, but he clearly felt awful about it, too—as he did about the suicides of Sean and Delilah. Although he appeared not to have fully accepted the deaths were self-inflicted and mentioned that Everett would be around again for a while to conduct an investigation.

"But that's not the main reason I wanted to see you," Casey said, staring at her earnestly.

Oh, no. What was to come? An admission of a girlfriend, a request that Melody keep their night of passion to herself? Something even worse?

"With all that's gone on, all we've been through together...well, I really like you, Melody. I'm not asking for any kind of commitment, but I'd like for us to go out together. On dates or whatever. Get to know each other better. And...see where it leads, if anywhere." He paused, reaching for her hands. "What do you think?"

"I think...yes!" Melody smiled, stood and held his hands tightly as she pulled him to his feet.

Okay, it was silly, meant nothing, but she pulled him to where the nearest sprig of mistletoe hung—and she kissed him.

No, he kissed her. They kissed each other—deeply and sexily and wonderfully. It was a long kiss, and Melody loved feeling his body hard against hers, his mouth searching hers.

And when they both pulled back, it was only for an instant. They kissed again.

"So we're on for your spending Christmas dinner with my family?" Casey said.

"Of course. But that's still weeks away. Can we see each other between now and then—on dates or whatever?"

"Absolutely," Casey said, then he bent toward her to seal that commitment with an even sexier kiss.

Dates together for the foreseeable future. And Christmas with his family.

No commitment, sure. But Melody felt overjoyed. Despite her misgivings before, the idea of having Casey in her life now, and maybe forever?

Delightful!

* * * * *

*Don't miss the books in Linda O. Johnston's
K-9 Ranch Rescue series:*

Trained to Protect
Second Chance Soldier

*All available now from
Harlequin Romantic Suspense!*

Get 4 FREE REWARDS!

We'll send you 2 FREE Books plus 2 FREE Mystery Gifts.

Harlequin® Romantic Suspense books feature heart-racing sensuality and the promise of a sweeping romance set against the backdrop of suspense.

FREE
Value Over
$20

YES! Please send me 2 FREE Harlequin® Romantic Suspense novels and my 2 FREE gifts (gifts are worth about $10 retail). After receiving them, if I don't wish to receive any more books, I can return the shipping statement marked "cancel." If I don't cancel, I will receive 4 brand-new novels every month and be billed just $4.99 per book in the U.S. or $5.74 per book in Canada. That's a savings of at least 12% off the cover price! It's quite a bargain! Shipping and handling is just 50¢ per book in the U.S. and $1.25 per book in Canada.* I understand that accepting the 2 free books and gifts places me under no obligation to buy anything. I can always return a shipment and cancel at any time. The free books and gifts are mine to keep no matter what I decide.

240/340 HDN GNMZ

Name (please print)

Address   Apt. #

City   State/Province   Zip/Postal Code

Mail to the **Reader Service:**
IN U.S.A.: P.O. Box 1341, Buffalo, NY 14240-8531
IN CANADA: P.O. Box 603, Fort Erie, Ontario L2A 5X3

Want to try 2 free books from another series? Call 1-800-873-8635 or visit www.ReaderService.com.

"What the hell are you doing?" she asked as she glanced
nervously around.

The curtains swished at the front window of her
parents' house. Someone was watching them.

"I'm trying to do my damn job," Hart said through
gritted teeth as he very obviously faked a grin.

She'd refused to let him inside the house last night.
From the dark circles beneath his eyes, he must not have
slept at all. Too bad his daughter's babysitter had arrived
at the agency before they'd left. He wouldn't have been
able to take Wendy home if he'd had to take care of
Felicity.

But even though his babysitter had shown up, the little
girl still needed her father—especially since he had full
custody. Where was her mother?

"You need a safer job," she told him.

"I'm fine," he said, but his voice lowered even more to a growl of frustration. "It's my assignment that's a pain in the ass."

She smiled—just as artificially as he had. "Then you need another assignment."

He shook his head. "This is the one I have," he said. "So I'm going to make the best of it."

Then he did something she hadn't expected. He lowered his head until his mouth brushed across hers.

Her pulse began to race and she gasped.

And he kissed her again, lingering this time—his lips clinging to hers before he deepened the kiss even more. When he finally lifted his head, she gasped again—this time for breath.

"What the hell was that?" she asked.

He arched his head toward the front window of the house. "For our audience…"

"You're overacting," she said—because she had to remind herself that was all he was doing. Acting…

He wasn't really her boyfriend. He wasn't really attracted to her. He was only pretending.

Don't miss
Evidence of Attraction *by Lisa Childs*
available December 2019 wherever
Harlequin® *Romantic Suspense*
books and ebooks are sold.

Harlequin.com

HRSEXP1119

Need an adrenaline rush from nail-biting tales
(and irresistible males)?

Check out **Harlequin Intrigue**®,
Harlequin® Romantic Suspense and
Love Inspired® Suspense books!

New books available every month!

CONNECT WITH US AT:

Facebook.com/groups/HarlequinConnection

 Facebook.com/HarlequinBooks

Twitter.com/HarlequinBooks

 Instagram.com/HarlequinBooks

Pinterest.com/HarlequinBooks

ReaderService.com

HARLEQUIN®

**ROMANCE WHEN
YOU NEED IT**

SGENRE2018R